"The................g
you'd better know."

Vic motioned toward a chair, and Amy
sat down.

"You may think that what I'm doing here
is just a fling," he began, "something I'll
tire of. Well, it's not. I have no intention
of going back to my former life-style.
That's over and done with."

Amy wanted to interrupt, but Vic's voice
was unrelenting.

"I don't give a damn about three-piece
suits and fancy cars. And if that's why
you fell in love with me, you'd better go
home. There's nothing for you here."

Amy was stunned. It wasn't the loss of
Vic's expensive life-style that had
crushed her dreams—it was the loss of
the gentle, lovable man he had once
been. But everything was changed
now—everything.

Love Beyond Reason

by

KAREN VAN DER ZEE

Harlequin Books

TORONTO • LONDON • LOS ANGELES • AMSTERDAM
SYDNEY • HAMBURG • PARIS • STOCKHOLM • ATHENS • TOKYO

Original hardcover edition published in 1980
by Mills & Boon Limited

ISBN 0-373-02406-1

Harlequin edition published May 1981

CHAPTER ONE

IT had been a terrible mistake; Amy realised it as soon as she saw Vic's face—hard and cold with anger. A shiver ran down her back and her legs felt wobbly. He didn't look at all like she remembered him. Was this really Vic, this stranger with the three-day growth of beard, the deep tan, the dusty old jeans? There was a squareness about the dark head, a hard muscularity about his body that she didn't recognise. Standing there in the middle of all those people wearing strange clothes—saris and turbans and veils—everything seemed unreal to her. Was this a nightmare? A hallucination? An optical illusion? She closed her eyes briefly, wanting to shut out the alien world around her, the strangeness of that big man in front of her. When she looked again he was still standing there, silent like a rock, with his feet slightly apart and his hands in his pockets, his eyes still angry. Amy felt sick and dizzy with everything around her swirling in mad circles.

No wonder! She hadn't seen a bed for over thirty hours and she was exhausted. The last few nights she had hardly slept at all, kept awake by excitement and the longing to see him again. Taking a deep breath, she anchored her feet to the floor to steady herself and bent down to pick up her suitcases. Her hair fell forward, blocking everything from view, and for a fleeting moment she wished she could hide for ever behind the dark curtain of hair. She straightened, tossing it back behind her shoulders with a swift movement of her head, and then Vic took a step forward, grabbed her by the arm, quite ungently, and swung her closer. The suitcases dropped from her fingers and she almost lost her balance.

'How the hell did you get it into that silly little head of yours to play a trick like this?' His voice was as hard as his eyes, but there was a curious, underlying note of something else she couldn't identify. His tight grip hurt her. She looked away, feeling again that dizziness overwhelming her. Before her eyes, the hustle and bustle of the airport terminal was a blurred mixture of colour and movement.

A trick? No, coming to Africa certainly was not intended as a trick. She had missed him terribly after he had gone to Kenya. She wanted to be with him, and in an impulsive moment she had booked a flight and packed her bags. In the weeks she had needed to get ready, she had only thought in positive terms. Vic would be glad to see her. He had missed her as much as she had missed him. It would be wonderful to be with him again. *She loved him.*

But this man standing here in front of her didn't even look like Vic, not the Vic she had known with a clean shaven face and impeccable clothes. She'd never seen him in faded jeans and a denim work shirt with the sleeves rolled up. She'd never seen those grey eyes look so angry.

'Did it ever occur to you that I might not receive your telegram? For your information, I'm gone for days at a time. I just got your cable this morning when I came back from safari. I nearly killed myself getting here and I barely made it. What if I hadn't? What would you have done here all by yourself?'

Amy swallowed. She felt weak with misery and fatigue and she suddenly yearned for her own bed in her New Jersey apartment, wishing she had never come. She licked her dry lips and forced herself to speak.

'I'm sorry. I'm terribly sorry. I ... I didn't think.'

His eyes blazed down on her. 'That's the whole trouble with you—you don't think! That impulsive head of yours is going to get you into big trouble one day! It nearly did this time!' He picked up her suitcases and without another word marched out of the airport.

Amy followed him meekly. He was right: impulsive she was. Things always happened to her because of it. She'd run the bath, then think of something else and leave the house and come back to find the place half flooded. And once, on the spur of the moment, she'd painted one of the walls in her kitchen green, only to find that she hated it the next day, that she never really liked that kind of green, that it destroyed her appetite.

And now this.

She blinked against the hard bright sunlight and quickly fished her sunglasses out of her handbag.

She'd never seen a Land Rover close up, let alone ridden in one. It was a strange vehicle for Vic to be driving and she was aware of the contrast once more. At home he'd had a sleek cream-coloured sports car, but this greenish monster was built for performance only. It was dusty and scratched up and she felt strangely out of place sitting next to Vic in a car like that. Everything seemed unreal, out of focus, somehow. Amy shook her head, trying to clear her mind, trying to shake the pieces back into place, but her confusion only became worse when they moved into the heavy city traffic. Strong brown hands on the wheel, Vic manoeuvred the Land Rover through a maddening maze of intersections and traffic circles, avoiding vehicles which seemed to come from all the wrong directions. Was she going crazy? Seeing double? A few fearful moments later she realised that traffic moved on the left, not on the right, and she sighed in relief. Maybe there was hope yet.

Caught in a bubble of silence they left Nairobi and drove along a narrow winding road through hills and lush green countryside. Swallowing uneasily, Amy looked at the familiar profile. The same strong features —the square chin jutting out a bit too much, the straight nose, the high forehead with the black hair blowing across it. Still there was a difference. The unshaven chin added a touch of strangeness, but she rather liked it in a way she couldn't explain. He looked rougher, less polished, more masculine. And more of a stranger.

He was staring straight ahead through dark glasses that hid his expression and he hadn't said a word since they'd left the airport. There was a tension in him, faint but discernible, increasing her own uneasiness. What was he thinking? Figuring out what to do with her now that she was here? Oh, God, she shouldn't have come. He didn't want her here. As the silence continued, she felt smaller and smaller, humiliation eating away at her self-confidence.

She had never thought about going to Africa, until suddenly it had hit her that there was no reason why she shouldn't. Being a nursery school teacher, she had a long vacation. She had enough money in her savings account. *Vic* was there. So why not?

Well, she'd just found out why not, hadn't she? What she'd done was burden Vic with the task of dealing with an unwanted female—*her.*

Suddenly he looked in her direction, scanning her quickly before turning his eyes back to the road.

'Tired?'

'Yes.'

'It's not too far.' His voice was calm. 'See those bushes over there? That's tea.'

'It's beautiful,' she said. And it was—thick and green, the bushes stretched out like a carpet. He went on pointing out other things—banana plants, pineapple. The soil next to the surfaced road was rusty red. Strange, she thought, red soil. Her eyes were heavy and for a while she dozed.

'This is Nyeri,' he said some time later. 'We're almost there now.'

Nyeri. A small town. Little shops and streets filled with people—African women carrying heavy loads on their backs, Indian women in saris, small children in raggedy clothes.

'I get my mail here,' said Vic, 'and I do most of my shopping here in town.' His anger seemed to have faded away and Amy was grateful.

The surfaced road ended and they followed a dirt track, red and dusty and uneven. Twenty minutes later they entered the village. To Amy it was like something from a television documentary—small round huts with peaked thatched roofs, a few cement buildings, dirt paths, and people everywhere. Little children shrieked and laughed, jumping on to the Land Rover as they bumped slowly through the village. Old women with bald heads, smooth and shiny as glass, stared at them. They wore bright orange or blue pieces of cloth slung over one shoulder and tied around their waists. Their earlobes were stretched out into thin strings of flesh hanging down to their shoulders and they looked frighteningly strange to Amy. There were younger women too, wearing flowered dresses with gathered skirts and scarves knotted on their heads. She felt more comfortable looking at them.

In his letters Vic had never gone into much description of his surroundings and Amy had not been able to conjure up a picture of the place where he lived. Now that she was here, in this African mud hut village, the reality of what she had done overwhelmed her. Her throat closed and she knew she had never been so frightened in her life. How could she have done such a stupid, impulsive thing? *Why* hadn't she given it more thought?

Vic stopped in front of a large house partially hidden behind green vegetation. It didn't look like any of the other buildings in the village.

'My castle,' he said with mockery in his voice. 'Used to be a colonial settler's house. Pretty fancy, once.'

The children had surrounded the car and were staring at Amy through the open window, only inches away. Some were shouting and laughing.

'*Jambo! Jambo! Jambo, memsahib!*'

In confusion she looked at Vic and she saw he was laughing at her.

'They're just being friendly,' he said. 'They're saying hello. Just say *jambo* back.'

She felt warm and uncomfortable and she wished they could just go into the house, but she knew that Vic was going to sit there until she had said hello.

'*Jambo,*' she said to the children, and they shrieked in laughter. Colour rose to her cheeks and she bit her lip.

'Very good,' said Vic. His face was cool and expressionless, the laughter gone. He jumped out of the Land Rover and said something to the children, which made them laugh even more. They moved away a few feet to let Amy get out. She was sure they were all laughing at her and helpless anger crept up inside her. At home she was good with children, knew how to handle them; it was her job. Here she was out of her element, not knowing a word of Swahili. Everything was different and she was a stranger. She felt like a fish in a canary cage, helpless and out of control.

The house was cool and dark. The room they entered was very large and had a huge fireplace, but there was very little furniture—some old chairs, a table, a bookcase. The worn wooden floor creaked under their feet.

At the far end of the room, a door opened and an African entered. '*Jambo, bwana, jambo, memsahib!*'

Vic introduced the man as Kariuki. 'He runs my life,' he said. 'Cooks, cleans, organises—and best of all, he's a great teacher.'

'Teacher?' she queried.

He nodded. 'Local affairs, customs, language—the works.'

'I see.' Amy smiled at Kariuki. He was short and thin and had a friendly, open face, and he reminded her of someone she knew who worked for McDonald's back home. To know that something—somebody—in this weird place reminded her of hamburgers and french fries was a comforting thought.

'Kariuki is also about to become a father for the first time,' Vic went on. 'His wife is due any day now.' He said something in Swahili to Kariuki, then took Amy's arm and led her into a dark hall. 'Let me show you your room.'

It was dark, like the rest of the place, with small windows and another fireplace. There was a bed with a mattress covered with a sheet and a striped sleeping bag. A table, a straight-backed chair, and a small chest of drawers completed the decor.

'I'm sorry I have no better accommodation to offer, but that's the way it is. I bought only the bare essentials when I came here. A Peace Corps allowance doesn't stretch very far. The furniture, by the way, is standard government stuff issued by the Ministry of Works.'

'It's fine,' she stammered. 'I ... I'm sorry I put you through all this trouble. It's so terribly stupid of me, I....' She felt close to tears and she turned away.

'We'll talk about it later. Why don't you rest for a while? Have a bath, whatever. Dinner should be ready in about an hour.' Vic sounded almost normal.

Amy nodded. 'Okay.'

'The bathroom is straight across from your room.' Vic stepped out into the hall and opened a door. 'Kariuki had a fire going under the water tank, so there should be some warm water for you if you want to wash.'

The bathroom fixtures were ancient. The bath tub looked as if all the enamel had been scrubbed off, and it probably was. Amy looked at it suspiciously.

Vic stood in the door watching her. 'It's all old, but

it's clean, so don't look as if you're scared you'll catch
some horrible disease.'

'I'm vaccinated.'

A faint smile twitched his lips. 'There's not much
water, so only use what you really need.' He left her
alone and Amy took another look around. There was
soap and a clean towel, all she needed, really. She
went back to her room and opened her suitcases, wondering what to wear. Flowered skirts, lacy blouses,
slinky dresses. In a place like this? No way. Vic had
liked her in feminine clothes, but who could tell what
he liked now? Or whether he even cared one way or
the other. Jeans and a T-shirt would have to do.

With her clothes draped over her arm and her bag
of toiletries in her hand, she went back to the bathroom. It didn't take her long to take a bath with the
little water she allowed herself. She dressed quickly,
creamed her face and brushed her hair. In the cracked
mirror above the sink she saw her face, drawn and
pale, her eyes too big and too dark. Brown hair,
brown eyes. What else could you expect, having Italian
grandparents? She was no beauty, she knew. But she
wasn't the Wicked Witch of the West, either, and
she knew that too. Her hair was thick and shiny, long,
very heavy, hanging down below her shoulders. But
it was straight. Dead straight. Not the slightest hint of
a curl, not the tiniest wave, not a one. She smoothed
it back and sighed. Well, she had a nice shape, she
supposed, all the right curves in all the right places,
but there was nothing particularly breathtaking about
her appearance. Wouldn't it be nice, she thought, to
wake up one day, look in the mirror and see something
really spectacular? A gorgeous face, a voluptuous body.
She'd always wished for at least one striking feature,
something that would make men turn around and take
a second look at her, but she wasn't sure what exactly
it should be. A bust size 38D? Bright red hair?
Good Lord, no!

But Vic had once called her beautiful, and she remembered the incident in every detail. Quickly she gathered her things and went back to her room, trying to block out the memory and the irony of it all. She lay down on the bed and closed her eyes. Vic's face floated through her mind, but it wasn't the face with the unshaven chin and the angry eyes. It was the old Vic with the smile on his face and the tenderness in his eyes as he looked at her. She even remembered, could still hear, the tone of his voice that night he had said she was beautiful, deep and warm and full of emotion.

He had taken her out in New York City for dinner and a play. They'd eaten at the restaurant on top of the World Trade Center—Windows on the World, and from the unfathomable heights, the city had looked like a sparkling miracle of lights. Literally and figuratively she'd been on top of the world. She felt wonderful, ecstatic, alive, and glowing like a Christmas tree. She always did when she was near Vic. There was something between them, something magical she'd never put into words. She'd only known him a few months, but he'd taken her out often, showing her New York and all its attractions. Although she'd lived in New Jersey for some years, she'd been to the city only on rare occasions.

Vic spent a fortune taking her out, but she knew he had it. He had lots of money; it was obvious in the way he dressed, the fancy sports car he drove, and his expensively furnished Manhattan apartment.

That night he drove her back to her apartment in New Jersey and she asked him in for a cup of coffee before he drove all the way back to the city.

In the kitchen they talked about the play they had seen and Amy made a joke, she couldn't remember what, and Vic laughed and laughed. Then suddenly he became serious, took her face in his hands and

looked into her eyes with such tenderness, she felt
weak with love.

'Amy, oh, Amy, you're beautiful.' Then he kiseed
her—slowly, thoroughly, gently. It was a kiss that
said more than a thousand words. It was a magic
moment, a moment when the truth became clear to
Amy: she loved him. It was more than just an innocent romance. It was something deep and real and
special.

'You're beautiful,' he whispered again. 'Everything
about you, inside and out.'

With a certainty beyond understanding she knew
that what he was really saying was that he loved her.
Standing there with his arms around her, she felt overwhelmed with love and happiness. She wanted to
stand there for ever.

'I don't want to leave,' Vic said huskily, as if he'd
read her thoughts. Her heart lurched and she felt his
arms tighten around her. 'But I will,' he added softly.

Her throat felt dry and she swallowed. 'Why?' She
wanted him to stay. Her whole being yearned for him,
all of him, and she didn't care whether it was right
or wrong, or if ever she'd be sorry.

He moved away a little, looking at her with dark,
serious eyes. 'You know why, Amy. I'm leaving for
Africa soon.'

Amy lay on top of the brown striped sleeping bag,
wishing she could ban the memories. Her whole body
seemed strangely keyed up and she couldn't relax.
Jet-lag probably, over-exhaustion.

Vic had been accepted by the Peace Corps shortly
after Amy had met him. It was the most incredible
thing about him. The Peace Corps was for idealistic
college kids, or so she had always thought. Not for
people like Victor Hoyt. He was thirty-four and had
built up a big engineering firm all by himself. He made
a lot of money and was successful in almost anything
he touched. Why did he want to join the Peace Corps,

live on a subsistence level in some poverty-stricken area
of the world? Vic, who liked good food, nice clothes
and all the luxury money could buy?

'I'm bored,' he'd told her. 'Plain bored. My business
is no challenge any more. I can set up another one,
but it would just be more of the same. I need a new
goal in life and I don't know what it is.' He made a
sweeping gesture around his apartment. 'But I do
know that all this isn't it. It means nothing to me
now that I have it.'

He had sold his company, his car and all his furniture and left for Africa.

Amy was miserable. He had never said that he loved
her, had made no commitments of any sort. He had
not asked her to wait for him, or join him, or anything that indicated his interest in keeping their
relationship going. Had she misread him? Was she
imagining love where none existed?

Not knowing was the worst of all. She had written
to him and he had answered her letters, but he hadn't
written what she wanted to hear—something personal,
something about his feelings for her. He had told her
about his work and his life generally, but not in great
detail. It was a world she didn't share with him and
didn't understand and each letter had made her feel
more out of touch with him, more desperate.

And now she was here, in his house, in this African
village with mud huts and strangely dressed people.
Now she was here and he was angry. He didn't want
her here. Vic seemed a stranger, a man she didn't recognise. But it couldn't be, it couldn't be....

There was a knock on the door and she got up to
open it. It was Vic, still dressed the same, in jeans
and work-shirt, but clean ones this time, and the
stubble on his chin was gone.

'Kariuki has dinner ready,' he said. 'Were you
asleep?'

She shook her head. 'No—I was too keyed up. Jet-lag, I imagine.'

'It will take a few days before you'll get back to normal.'

There was a bowl of stew on the table—meat, peas, beans, carrots. Amy wondered what kind of meat and some gruesome possibilities entered her mind. Don't ask, she told herself. Just eat. Chew, swallow, don't taste.

Calm grey eyes observed her. 'Don't look so suspicious. It's just mutton stew, nothing more exotic than that.'

Mutton. *Sheep*. Next to what she'd been thinking, it was nothing. She'd eaten lamb, but never mutton, but it was good and she ate a big helping. She remembered the meals they had eaten together in classy restaurants in New York—how different this dinner was! Not that it mattered in any important sense—all she really cared about was being with Vic, seeing the crinkly lines around his eyes when he smiled, hearing his deep resonant laughter, listening to him talk. That was what she had been looking forward to, and more, but it wasn't the way she had expected it to be.

Vic spoke very little while he ate and the atmosphere seemed filled with an awkwardness and unease that she had no power to disperse. Words fell like heavy weights in the silence and the strangeness of him kept her from talking freely to him, the way she used to. It didn't seem right to say the things she wanted to say, things she could have said when they were still together in the States.

Kariuki cleared the table and came back from the kitchen with two lanterns which he placed near the fireplace. It was only six and already darkness was falling. It was cooler now too. Vic stood up from his chair and went to the fireplace and lit the wood that had already been put there.

'Make yourself comfortable,' he said, pointing at one of the chairs near the fire. 'There are books over there if you want to read. Reading is about all I do for entertainment. There is nothing else.' He took a book himself and sat down.

Amy scanned the titles on the shelves—works on well digging and water systems, on economic and social development, and a variety of other non-fiction books. There were paperback novels too. In the end she found a Swahili textbook and took it off the shelf and went back to the fireplace. She leafed through the book. *Jambo*—Hello. *Habari?*—How are you?

Would it be hard to learn? But what use would it be? She'd be on a plane back to New York in a few days. She shivered suddenly and moved the chair closer to the fire. Vic looked up from his book.

'Would you like some coffee?'

'Oh, yes, please.' Amy jumped up. 'I'll make it.'

'Okay. Take your lamp. The coffee and the sugar are in the meat safe—that's that screened cupboard. And there's milk in the fridge.'

'You have a fridge? I thought there was no elec-tricity in the house.'

'There isn't.' He looked at her with humour in his eyes. 'It runs on kerosene.'

'Oh.' Feeling dumb, she walked out of the room, carrying the lamp in front of her. She'd never heard of a refrigerator running on anything but electricity.

The house looked sinister in the sparse light of her lamp. The kitchen was at the far end of the hall, as if it had been built on as an afterthought. It looked more like a garden shed than anything else, with the corrugated iron roof simply laid over the wooden beams. There was a cement floor and plain wood sid-ing. A small cast iron wood stove stood on one wall and across from it was a sink, but no taps. A large ceramic tank stood on a rough wooden table and she realised it must be the water filter Vic had mentioned earlier.

She found little white cups, sugar, milk, instant coffee. She filled the kettle with water from the filter and put it on a gas ring. A large tank of gas stood behind it. It all looked so primitive, she could hardly have pictured it in her imagination.

When the water boiled she filled the cups and took the milk and sugar along to the sitting room. Vic always drank his coffee black, but it had been a long time ago since she had last had coffee with him. A long time and a whole world away.

'You still drink your coffee black?'

He looked up from his book, eyebrows raised. 'Yes, sure. Why not?'

Because everything else has changed, she wanted to say. *Because you're not the same. You look so different and you act like a stranger*. Instead she shrugged lightly. 'Just wondering.'

She sat down on the soft white sheepskin in front of the fire and stared into the flames while she drank her coffee. The silence between them made her more and more uncomfortable, but she didn't know what to say any more. How was it possible that they couldn't talk together any more? It had always been so easy. Memories. Memories of long, lazy evenings of wine and music and the sharing of their thoughts and impressions flowed into her consciousness.

Absorbed in thoughts, she was not aware of time or surroundings and she started when suddenly Vic sat down next to her on the sheepskin.

'Sorry, didn't mean to scare you.'

Amy said nothing. She kept her eyes on the fire, her heart racing crazily. He took her hand and held it.

'What are you thinking about?'

She swallowed. She couldn't look at him. 'I was thinking how strange everything is. It's not the way I expected it to be.'

'It's not what I expected, either.'

She gave him a quick glance. A faint smile curved his lips, but she couldn't read his eyes. She didn't know what he meant. Had he expected his life here to be different? Or had he not expected her to be here?

His hand was warm on hers and his closeness disturbed her, made a deep longing flow through her body like warm wine.

'Don't look away, Amy.' He took her face in his hands and turned it towards him. She lowered her eyes, aware of the pounding of her heart, praying he wouldn't notice.

'Look at me, Amy!' There was an urgent note in his voice and when she looked at him she saw his eyes, dark and questioning.

He kissed her then and it was like it had been. Her fear fell away and she put her arms around his neck and held him tightly. This was the Vic she remembered, full of warmth and tenderness. Everything else was forgotten—the village, the old house, his anger at her coming, the strangeness of him. All she knew was his touch and the sensuous feeling of his body against hers, his mouth on hers.

He moved away slowly, looking at her, smiling. 'This is what you came here for, isn't it?'

Yes, she wanted to say, *I love you and I missed you so*. But suddenly the dream fell away and she was back in the mud hut village in the arms of a stranger.

Here it comes now, she thought miserably. He's going to tell me I've made a mistake, that I shouldn't have come. And he'll be *very* nice and *very* gentle, of course, telling me that what we had at home belonged in a different time, a different place.

She rallied her pride and her courage, knowing there was a way out, and managed a small smile, she knew not how.

'I'm on vacation,' she said slowly. 'I wanted to see

Kenya and I hoped you wouldn't mind putting me up for a little while.'

There was a brief silence and then he laughed out loud, but she didn't like the way it sounded. He wasn't amused. His reaction confused her and the hollow, angry sound of his laughter filled her with apprehension. He pulled her close again and kissed her, but there was no tenderness now, only selfish, insensitive demand. She stiffened in response to his total lack of gentleness and struggled against him without result.

'Relax,' he whispered. 'Relax.' His hands moved under her shirt, reaching for her breasts, and she gasped in fear at his deliberately offensive manner. She didn't know this man—this cold, callous male. There was no doubting what he intended to do and she didn't want it—not in this hostile, unfeeling way.

'Let me go!' She pushed against his chest with every ounce of strength in her, and when Vic suddenly let her go she lost her balance and almost fell backward.

'You almost convinced me, but not quite.' There was cold contempt in his voice.

Trembling helplessly, Amy glared at him, feeling only a hot fury now. 'What's got into you? You never behaved like this at home ... like some ... some kind of animal!'

His laugh was short and dry. 'At home I was nice and polite and a perfect gentleman, is that what you're saying?'

'Yes.' It wasn't exactly that, though, she thought miserably. It wasn't *what* he'd done, but the *way* he'd done it, that lack of love in his touch, his cold aggression.

'When we met at home,' he said without much expression, 'I knew I was leaving soon. I decided it wouldn't be fair to either of us to get involved too deeply.'

'But it's fair now?'

His lips twisted. 'Look around you, sweetheart. We're far away from home and all alone in the bush. You presented yourself to me on a silver platter. What do you expect me to do?'

Amy was still shaking and she couldn't stop. 'You could control yourself, act normally!' Oh, God, she thought, I sound like a prudish spinster.

Vic threw his head back and laughed. 'Honey, I'm as normal as they come. Why do you suppose I want to sleep with you?'

'I don't care! I want you to leave me alone!' Amy got to her feet, but he grabbed her arm and pulled her back on to her knees.

'I'm warning you,' he said slowly. 'Don't expect me to act like a saint. If you want to use my house as a hotel while you're on vacation, you're welcome to. But you'll have to accept the consequences!'

CHAPTER TWO

VIC let her go and without another word Amy rose to her feet and left the room, making as dignified an exit as was possible under the circumstances. She threw herself on the bed and lay there trembling, her eyes tightly shut. Was this a nightmare after all? Or the preview to an X-rated movie? Vic had never behaved as he had tonight, and neither had she, for that matter. Never before had she resisted his advances—she *loved* him, she wanted him, and it had been Vic who'd set the limits: *'You know why, Amy, I'm leaving for Africa soon.'*

What had changed that kind and gentle man into that rough and brutal male? He had always been considerate of her feelings, treating her as if she were someone very special—very special indeed. Like truffles, she thought miserably, very special, very dispensable.

What had got into him? Was it the water? The climate? Maybe living in these primitive conditions had brought out the beast in him, given him Stone Age urges. Next thing she knew he'd be dragging her around by the hair.

It was cold and Amy shivered. How could it be cold in Africa? Well, there were a few things to learn, or so it seemed. She had the ominous feeling that before she left Africa she'd be a lot wiser, if not happier. She prepared for bed and crawled into the sleeping bag, wrapping it tightly around her and pulling it up to her chin. Let him try and get her out of this!

Damn, she thought, why am I hurting like this? She had dreamed, longed, fantasised about this night, the night of her arrival. Oh, God, she moaned, I wish

I were dead. 'No, I don't,' she said out loud, and took a deep breath. So she had been wrong. So she had made a mistake. It was not the end of the world. There were worse disasters than a broken heart— floods, earthquakes, revolutions, to mention a few; starvation, disease, poverty, to mention some more. I could have been born blind, she thought cheerfully, or ugly, or with a club foot.

When self-pity struck, thinking up miseries worse than her own sometimes helped, as if with them she could exorcise her own hurt and pain. This time it didn't work.

Like a child, she cried herself to sleep.

She had a terrible night, her sleep restless with images of bald-headed women, curious children and Vic's savage face with an unholy grin and a bushy black beard. It was almost nine when she awoke, feeling like a dirty rag and looking even worse. What she needed was about a week's solid sleep, preferably in a silent convent on the other side of the globe. Nuns had it made, she thought. She brushed her teeth, spattering toothpaste on the mirror.

Outside the world was bright and sunny and very still. Inside, the house was dark and gloomy, matching her mood. It was an enormous structure with many large rooms, a perfect set for a horror movie, the huge fireplaces just right for human sacrifice. Amy roamed through the empty rooms, listening to the hollow sound of her footsteps echoing off the ceilings. By the looks of it, Vic only lived in the guest wing and the rest of the place was unused.

Back in the living room, she decided to make herself some coffee, when out of nowhere Kariuki appeared. Gesturing enthusiastically and speaking half in Swahili and half in English, he explained that he would get her some breakfast.

She noticed that the table was set for one. Vic must have left for work. Good: she didn't feel like facing him just yet. A clucking sound made her turn and she saw a mother hen and her brood casually enter the front door and head for the table with unequalled audacity. Busily picking up crumbs, they ignored her totally and completely. Kariuki came in with a tray and chased the chickens out, grinning at Amy with an easy shrug as if to say, 'Well, what can you do?' Amy liked him. He had a humorous glint in his eyes, and although they couldn't say more than a few words to each other, she felt at ease with him.

A car rolled up to the house just as she finished her food, and the next moment Vic strode through the door, eyes cool.

'I see you're up,' he commented.

'I'm up.'

Without another word or look he disappeared into the hall, coming back a few minutes later with a small canvas bag. With her elbows on the table she was sipping her coffee and when their eyes met all she saw was a dark misty grey, clouded, unreadable. He wound his watch without taking his eyes off her.

'I apologise for my behaviour last night,' he said, looking stony cold, alien, distant.

Amy glared back at him, equally stony, or so she hoped. He didn't move. She didn't speak. Was he waiting? For what? A standing ovation?

'I said, I apologise,' he repeated.

'And I thank you. From the bottom of my heart.'

His teeth clenched together, his jaw muscles tensed. It gave her a strange satisfaction to watch him try to control his anger. He picked up his bush hat and jammed it on top of his head with a vicious gesture.

'You'll be relieved to know that I won't be here to-night and possibly not tomorrow night, either.'

'Hallelujah!'

He grabbed his bag and strode out of the room, ignoring her remark. Then suddenly reality struck and panic surged through her. *I don't want to be alone!* she thought fiercely. *I don't want to be alone in this godforsaken place tonight!* She almost ran after him, stood in the door as he swung himself in the driver's seat and threw his bag in the back of the Land Rover. She swallowed hard.

'Do you *have* to leave?'

He looked at her coldly. 'I have a job to do. I move around a lot. The roads are bad and it's dark early; I just can't make it home every day. If you'd expected me to act as your tour guide, I'll have to disappoint you.' He started the engine and slowly bumped down the dirt track.

Bereft of speech, Amy stared after him. He did not look back. She felt overwhelmed with fear at the prospect of being alone at night in this gloomy house in the African bush with no one around who could understand her.

She struggled through the day, not knowing what to do with herself. She wandered around in the garden, not being able to conjure up enough courage to venture out into the village. She wasn't quite ready to encounter bald ladies with stringy earlobes. The garden had gone totally wild, but remnants of its former beauty were still there. She found clumps of pretty flowers that looked like lilies and profusely blooming bushes she didn't know by name. Once an English settler's family must have lived here and she could imagine how pretty everything must have looked and how beautiful the house with polished floors and nice furniture. As she wandered around, she came upon Kariuki who was pulling weeds in a vegetable garden. So Vic was even eating his own homegrown vegetables. The contrast was there again. The sophisticated Manhattan business man she had once known seemed to disappear more and more into oblivion.

At four o'clock the sky suddenly turned dark and without much warning the rain came pelting down. The world turned dark and damp and Amy shivered in the sudden cold and wondered if she should light the fire. Well, that was what it was there for, wasn't it?

As she put a match to the paper and kindling, Kariuki entered the room carrying a tray which he put down near the fireplace.

'*Chai*,' he said, pointing at the teapot.

'Thank you,' Amy answered. '*Asante sana*,' she corrected bravely, remembering the words from the Swahili textbook.

Kariuki smiled broadly. '*Mzuri sana!*'

Amy felt ridiculously pleased, as if she'd accomplished something quite miraculous. She poured herself a cup of tea and watched the flames licking their way around the logs. Night was not far off and her imagination ran riot, uncontrollably, conjuring up bloodcurdling scenes in which she herself played the leading role of helpless victim. When the knock on the door came she jumped, then froze. The door flew open and a girl made her entrance, a blue towel covering her head and shoulders. Amy stared at the dripping shape—tight blue jeans, red T-shirt under a heavy unbuttoned cardigan, short hair, very large blue eyes that looked at her in surprise.

'Hi,' she said. 'Is Vic home?'

'No,' Amy replied automatically, standing up from her chair. 'He left this morning. He'll be gone a couple of days.'

The girl pulled the towel off her head. 'Oh.' Then her face broke out into a smile, showing a beautiful set of teeth. 'I'm sorry, I'm behaving like a clod. I'm Tanya Palmer.'

Amy's heart had returned to its normal rhythm and she was breathing calmly again. 'I'm Amy Morelli.'

'I'm just stopping by to drop off Vic's towel. He left it at my house the other day.' Tanya handed Amy the soaked towel. 'Sorry it got wet. Are you a P.C.V.?'

Was she a *what*? P.C.V.—Potential Crime Victim? Poor Confused Virgin? That was her all right.

'P.C.V.?' she queried.

'Peace Corps Volunteer.' Tanya grinned. 'Obviously the answer is no.' Nice grin, friendly face.

'I'm on vacation here,' said Amy.

There was a momentary silence and a sudden guarded look came into the girl's eyes.

'I see. Well, I've got to run—my ride is waiting. Say hi to Vic when he gets back.' She walked out into the rain. *'Kwa heri!'*

Amy stood frozen, eyes glued to the wet towel in her hands. Tanya Palmer. Who was she? And what was one of Vic's towels doing in her house? Take three guesses, she told herself.

It only took one.

Amy sank down into her chair. Her throat felt dry and a sickening feeling of despair filled her. It was all clear now. All the bits and pieces added up to a very neat package. She knew now why Vic had been so furious when he'd picked her up at the airport, why he hadn't wanted her to come at all. Why had it never occurred to her that he might find someone in Kenya? Like a fool she'd been dreaming about him, longing for him, thinking of him. And he? He'd probably not given her much thought, considered her a pleasant memory at best. Maybe he was into passing affairs and temporary attachments. She belonged to the past and was too far away. Tanya was a reality close at hand.

Could she blame him? He had never said he loved her, promised her nothing, asked nothing. He had treated her fairly and she herself was to blame for what she was going through now. Blindly she stared into the flames, feeling nothing of the fire's warmth, only a cold misery seeping through her veins. How could she have been so naïve? Her throat ached with the effort not to cry, her eyes burned. With trembling hands she picked up her cup and finished her tea. It tasted like dirty dishwater.

There was no time to contemplate the issue as she

heard a car slithering to a stop in front of the house. Was the village as isolated as she'd thought? Maybe that dirt track was a major road between towns—it sure could have fooled her. Opening the door, she found a man standing in the rain, a face full of freckles and hair plastered to his head. She moved aside to let him in.

'Good afternoon,' he said in a sing-song accent. (Danish? Swedish?) 'My name is Gunnar Hornsrud.' He extended his hand and Amy introduced herself. Question marks as big as the Empire State Building were visible in his blue eyes. Obviously, finding an unknown female in Vic's house was cause for surprise.

'I'm a friend of Vic's,' Amy explained. 'I'm here on vacation.' She didn't know what made her say that, why she had this need to justify her presence. She didn't owe this man any explanations.

He smiled. 'Kenya is a wonderful place for a holiday, although on a day like this one wouldn't say so.' He slid out of his wooden clogs, leaving them near the door, and moved to the fire and rubbed his hands. He was tall and painfully thin, stooping a little. Mid-twenties, she guessed.

He straightened and smiled. 'I came to ask Vic to come over for dinner on Saturday. One of the Peace Corps nurses in town is going back home and we're having a little farewell party for her. My wife is cooking some Norwegian food. If you're staying here, please come and join us too.'

'That's terribly nice of you, but I can't say ... I mean, I don't know what Vic's plans are. He may not be back here until Saturday.' And the last thing he'd probably want was to take her to a party and explain her presence to the world. 'Would you like a cup of tea?' she added quickly. 'I have this whole pot here and there's just me.'

'Oh, yes, please. That would be nice.' He lowered his skinny frame into a chair and put his long legs nearly into the fire. 'I'm wet and frozen.'

There was only one cup on the tray, so she went to the kitchen to get another.

'Are you Norwegian?' she asked him when she returned.

He nodded. 'My wife and I are both volunteers—the Norwegian equivalent of the Peace Corps. She's an instructor at the teachers' college and I'm a vet.'

She poured him a cup of tea. He took it from her, sloshed in a generous amount of milk and added four heaping spoons of sugar. He grinned at her astonished face.

'I like it sweet,' he said rather unnecessarily.

'No kidding?' His grin was infectious and she smiled. 'Do you like it here?'

'Oh, yes,' he said with genuine enthusiasm. 'But it was quite an adjustment at first.'

'I'm finding that out, too. I just got here yesterday.'

He stared at her wide-eyed. '*Yesterday?* And Vic left you alone already?'

'He had to go. And he ... he didn't know I was coming. Bad timing, that's all.'

'Kariuki is here, isn't he? Are you all right by yourself?'

A real human being, this one.

'Kariuki is here, and I'm fine,' she lied. 'It's all a little strange, of course, but that's all.' It was an understatement to end all understatements.

There was a short silence and over the edge of his cup Gunnar Hornsrud looked at her intently.

'Are you frightened?' he asked.

No, she wasn't frightened. She was terrified, panic-stricken.

'Should I be?'

He smiled. 'No, you're quite safe, but emotions don't always match the facts. For the first few days my wife was as jittery as a bowlful of jelly.'

So she wasn't the only one. 'I have to admit this

place gives me the creeps,' she said, 'but I'll get used to it.'

He poured himself more tea, added milk and sugar and sat back again. 'You'd better come to town with me, then. You can stay with us until Vic gets back. He'll come to town for the party on Saturday anyway.'

'Oh, no! That's not necessary!' Had he thought she'd been fishing for the invitation? 'It's terribly nice of you, but I'll manage, really.'

He didn't believe a word of it, she could see by the way he smiled.

'Listen,' he said, 'Africa is better taken in small doses. Being stuck by yourself in a spooky house in a mud hut village full of bald Kikuyu *mamas* isn't the way to do it.'

'I can't just drop in on your wife,' she said lamely.

'Inger likes company. People drop in all the time— that's the way it goes here. Don't worry about it.'

Amy hesitated. It was a tempting invitation. She might *be* safe, but she sure didn't *feel* safe. Well, who needed to be brave?

Gunnar stirred his tea extensively as if to make sure he got the full effect of every single grain of sugar. 'Well, are you coming?' he asked.

'It's really no trouble?'

'Not in the least. You can get your things now and I shall talk to Kariuki and tell him the plans. I'll leave a message for Vic.'

The rain had eased off a little, but the dirt road had changed into a mud bath. Slithering and sliding, they moved through the slippery muck, Amy fearfully holding on to the frame of the Volkswagen buggy. She sighed with relief when they finally reached the tarmac and Gunnar smiled at her sideways.

'That black cotton is terrible stuff, hard as cement when it's dry, soup when it's wet. No joke when you get stuck in it.'

He didn't have to convince her. She visualised the

scene, seeing herself stranded in the middle of nowhere with a perfect stranger.

It hit Amy suddenly in what a strange situation she found herself. Less than an hour ago she had not known this man. She had got into a car with him and he was taking her home to his wife, or so he said. Only the thought of this happening at home was outrageous. You didn't trust strangers just like that, and you most certainly didn't get into a car with one. Two days since she'd left the States and she was doing things she'd never dreamed of. This was a different world with its own rules and laws. Unsurreptitiously she glanced at Gunnar. He looked trustworthy enough, harmless, like a skinny teddybear. Not that that meant much; the prisons were full of harmless-looking individuals.

'Say,' she said, 'do you often pick up strange girls and take them home to your wife?'

'Only on Thursdays,' he said, and grinned.

Gunnar's home was a small house just out of Nyeri, containing the same standard government-issue furniture that Vic's place had. It also contained a wife, just like he had said, open and friendly like her husband and speaking with the same sing-song intonation.

'We're having soup and pancakes for dinner tonight,' Inger told Amy. 'Not a standard American combination, I've been told,' she added with a laugh.

Amy could feel her spirits rise as the evening progressed, gloom lifting like fog. It was good to be away from that big old house and the depressing reality of her situation. She went to bed early, slept for twelve hours straight and woke up feeling as if she'd risen from the dead. Her body was recuperating, and if her emotions would do the same she'd be in fine shape.

Inger was in the kitchen baking cookies. Gunnar had left for work hours ago, she said, and what would Amy like to eat? Eggs? Would she like to try some Norwegian goat cheese? What did she prefer—coffee or

tea? She fed Amy breakfast as if she were a valued
guest, a long-lost friend. In the afternoon she took her
out into town to show her around and to do some
shopping for the next day's party.

Many of the small shops were owned by Indian
traders and as they walked along the streets the
fragrance of incense spilled out on to the sidewalk.
The grocery store they entered was filled with the
smells of strong, exotic spices. Whatever Amy had
imagined Africa to be, this was not part of the picture
and again a sense of confusion began to cloud her
mind.

It was like one of those strangely muddled-up dreams
—fragments of truth oddly distorted, images of familiar people in mysterious places, garbled conversations,
mixed up time sequences. And in this alien world she
wandered around, searching for the man she loved, a
man with a clean-shaven face, gentle hands and a laugh
in his eyes. But what she had found was a rugged
man in dirty work clothes, with an angry look in his
eyes and arms that had held her without tenderness.

Two African women were sitting in front of the
grocery store selling vegetables and fruits from large
baskets. They wore flowered dresses and scarves knotted on their heads, like the younger women in the
village.

'*Jambo, memsahib,*' they said to Inger, repeating the
greeting to Amy.

Inger bought a large pineapple, tomatoes, passion
fruits and mangoes, laughing and haggling with the
women in Swahili. Then she loaded her purchases in
a sisal basket and handed it to Amy. 'If you don't
mind carrying this, I'll take the box from the store. I
think I've got everything I need. Let's get some
samosas and have tea with the nurses.'

Was everything that casual here? Husbands taking
home strange girls, people dropping in on friends with
an unknown person in tow? Apparently that was the

way it went. Absentmindedly Amy listened to Inger prattling about the nurses as they walked down the street.

'Cindy is the shy one,' Inger told her. 'She's leaving next week. And Bunny....' She grinned. 'Bunny you have to meet!'

They found both of them home in their modern two-storey apartment, reading their mail. Bunny—a face full of humour, light brown hair tortured into a frenzied frizz. She was barefoot and wore a dramatic kaftan made of bright orange material. She bounced up from her chair and took the offered bag of *samosas*.

'Tea! Tea coming up.' She sailed into the kitchen and Amy heard water running, the clatter of cups, and then Bunny's voice, singing some popular tune, loud and slightly off key.

Next to Bunny's vibrant personality, Cindy seemed to fade into the background. Small, shy and silent, she reminded Amy of a frightened little mouse. Obviously there had to be more to her than her appearance seemed to portray. Frightened little mice didn't join the Peace Corps.

There was a knock on the door. 'Cindy! Bunny!' The door flew open and in came Tanya, blue eyes bright, wide mouth smiling. 'Hi, everybody.' As she noticed Amy, there was again that guarded look clouding her eyes, an almost indiscernible fear.

'You haven't met Amy yet, have you?' Inger asked.

'We met at Vic's house yesterday,' she said, her voice calm, but there was a tightness about her mouth that didn't escape Amy's attention.

'You want to stay for tea and *samosas*?' Cindy asked. Her voice was as soft and colourless as the rest of her.

'I'd love to, but I can't stay long. I'm on my way to Nairobi. I just have to ask Bunny something—she's in the kitchen, I hear.' Her expression conveyed extreme suffering. 'When is she going to send that voice for a tune-up?' She swept into the kitchen and Amy could hear the two of them laughing and talking.

'What's the matter with you?' It was Bunny's voice. 'You have *mould* on your brain? Think! Think!'

A minute later they both came back to the living room with the tea tray, laughing helplessly.

For the next hour or so Amy listened to the conversation around her, not joining in very much. She watched Tanya, looking for signs ... signs of what? She didn't know. Something to give her an indication of her relationship with Vic—if there was one.

There was one, she knew. If only for a fleeting moment she had seen it in Tanya's eyes—yesterday, and again today. But there was nothing now. She was talking to Amy in a perfectly normal voice, saying perfectly normal things. She was a teacher, she said, in an up-country boarding school for girls. She liked Kenya. She liked peanut butter sandwiches, rabbits, and walking in the rain. She was nice, Amy had to admit to herself, and she wondered why it surprised her. Then it hit her. Of course! You weren't supposed to like your competition. The 'other woman' was supposed to be a miserable creature with long red fingernails, a husky voice and a voluptuous body—a femme fatale dressed to kill and smelling like a roomful of roses.

'Tell me,' Bunny said to Amy, 'what's brought you here? A man? A vacation? Both?'

Everyone looked at her, except Tanya, who was carefully stirring her tea, staring down into the cup with great interest.

How many more times would she have to go through this? Before the week was out she'd be an accomplished actress. Or *liar* was maybe a more accurate description.

She pasted on a smile. 'I'm on vacation,' she said as casually as she could manage. 'I'm staying with Vic for just a little while to get my bearings, and then I'd like to go to the game parks, see some more of the country. I suppose I'll have to go to Nairobi to book a safari.' She took a bite from her *samosa*, chewed, swallowed and gasped. The triangular pastry shell was filled with a spicy mixture that burned her tongue and throat. An Indian delicacy, Inger had said. What she hadn't said was that it was more like torture to the uninitiated palate. Amy gulped down her tea and wiped her watery eyes. They were laughing at her, pouring her more tea, assuring her that she'd learn to like the things soon enough.

Amy finished the *samosa* she still held in her hand, then had another one without blinking an eye. Not so bad after all. Pretty tasty. There were a lot of adjustments to be made. This one she might as well get out of the way.

Vic arrived early at the party the next evening, and Amy was alone in the living room when he made his entrance. An indefinable emotion penetrated her consciousness. Tall and powerful, he seemed to fill the room. For a timeless moment his eyes held hers.

'Hi there,' he said coolly, dumping his bag on the floor.

He was covered with red dust. Amy's eyes slowly took in his dishevelled appearance from the dusty work boots, the faded jeans, the casually buttoned shirt that showed the dark curly hair of his chest, to his face with another two days' growth of beard. He looked just like when she had first seen him at the airport—a stranger.

He took off his bush hat and looked at her with faint amusement.

'Not exactly the way you used to see me, is it?'

Three-piece suits, designer shirts, thirty-dollar ties, Italian shoes. Not even close.

'So it's really you, after all?' she said. 'I keep thinking I got myself mixed up in a case of mistaken identity.'

'It's me,' he said lightly. 'Or what's left of me, anyway.'

Inger entered the room, drying her hands on a kitchen towel. 'Hello, Vic. Glad you could make it. Did you find Gunnar's message?'

'Yes, thanks.'

Inger looked at Amy. 'What's the matter with you?'

'It's the shock of seeing me,' Vic answered for her. 'She knew me in my former life and she isn't used to the metamorphosis yet.' He was talking to Inger, but his eyes, full of derision, were on Amy.

Inger laughed and it seemed to come from a long distance. 'You'd better go and have a shower, Vic. You know the way.'

'Yes, thanks.' Vic disappeared to the bathroom and Amy followed Inger back into the kitchen.

'We have a communal bathroom,' Inger explained. 'All those poor souls living in the bush without proper water systems come to town to take baths. Cindy and Bunny get a fair share of them too. Vic is one of the few who pick up after themselves, brings his own things. A lot of these other guys assume I'll supply them with towels and soap and shampoo, and clean their bathtub rings when they're finished.'

Amy grimaced. 'That's disgusting!'

'It certainly is. Especially because some of these guys have been roaming the bush and haven't seen water for days.'

'Is there anything I can do to help?' Amy asked. 'You're doing all the work and I'm just standing here.'

'No, no. Joseph is coming any minute now. He'll finish up. He doesn't like people hanging around in the kitchen when he's busy.'

'Well, if you're sure, I'll go to my room and put my things away. That way I won't have to do it at the last moment.'

It didn't take long to put her clothes in her overnight case. She tidied the room and looked around to see if there was anything else she had forgotten. In front of the mirror she caught sight of her reflection and automatically picked up her brush and tidied her hair. There was a knock on the half-open door and in the mirror she saw Vic standing there, watching her. The dust and dirt had gone and so had the stubble on his chin. He looked strikingly handsome in just his simple sports clothes, brown pants, a light beige polo shirt contrasting with his dark tan.

'May I come in?' he asked.

She nodded, putting down her brush, her hand suddenly trembling. Again that feeling, more overpowering than before—her whole body, her mind, her soul, everything reacting to his presence.

He closed the door behind him. Amy didn't move, could not move as he came behind her, putting his hands on her shoulders, searching for her face in the mirror.

'I didn't know you were afraid to stay by yourself,' he said quietly. 'I should have thought about it.'

Amy averted her eyes. 'It doesn't matter.' She could feel the warmth of his body, his breath brushing her cheek.

'Why didn't you tell me?'

She shrugged, still not looking at him. 'I don't know ... I just didn't.'

His hands slowly moved to her neck, his fingers softly caressing her skin as they slid around to her throat.

'I see you're wearing my necklace.'

Ripples of warm longing surged through her at the feel of his touch. She swallowed. 'Yes. I like it.' Vic had given her the necklace as a goodbye present before he left. It was a simple, single coil of gold—no pendant, no fancy shiny stones, and she liked the honest simplicity of it. She had never cared much for jewellery, finding most of it pretentious or gaudy, but this chain was one of the few things she really liked. Her eyes met his in the mirror and she saw he was smiling.

'I knew you'd like it when I bought it. You're not the kind of girl who goes for diamonds and rubies, are you?'

'No.'

She still remembered every detail of that last evening, could still hear the empty, toneless sound of his voice when he called her on the phone. 'I'm coming to say goodbye.'

She noticed the strain in him as soon as he entered her apartment. He didn't want to go anywhere, he said. Would she mind if he called a restaurant and had a meal delivered? He threw his jacket on a chair and pulled off his tie. He opened a bottle of wine and poured some for both of them. Amy set the table, lit some candles and put a record on the stereo, all with a dull sense of futility. The mood was not there and the room itself seemed to be permeated with sadness.

The food was tasteless, like an economy TV dinner, flat, plastic. She could hardly swallow, couldn't even look at Vic as he sat across from her. The last time, she thought. The last time he'll be here with me.

When she came back from the kitchen with the coffee he was standing near the window looking out. He turned around. 'Come here, Amy. I have something for you.'

She put down the tray, walked over to him with stiff legs, took the little box from him. Too big for a ring.

I don't want any damn jewellery! she thought hysterically. *I want you!*

It was a necklace, a thick chain of shimmering gold. As he put it around her neck, his hands were warm against her skin. He kissed her lightly. His behaviour was strange and distant as if in spirit he had already left. All through dinner Amy had felt the remoteness in his manner.

'Thank you for the good times we've had together, Amy.'

It was all he said, but she wanted to hear more. Why didn't he tell her he loved her? That he would come back to her? She wanted to cry out with the pain and anguish that filled her. Overwhelmed with nameless fear, she stared at him, the dark hair, the strong familiar features of his face. I'm going to lose him, she thought. He's leaving me for another life, another world. He doesn't know I love him and I don't know how to tell him.

She put her arms around him, clung to him, never wanting to let him go. 'Thank you,' she whispered, 'thank you for the lovely necklace.' But it wasn't the necklace that was on her mind. She kissed him, kissed him with a desperate hunger she didn't know how to still. 'Hold me, Vic. Please hold me.'

He groaned, gently releasing her arms from their grip. 'Oh, my God, Amy, don't. Please, don't.' There was despair in his voice, anguish in his eyes and she knew why, only didn't understand why he didn't say the words she wanted to hear.

'Why are you looking so sad?'

She was in Africa, alone with him in this room, but everything between them had changed. His hands were still on her throat, fingering the gold chain.

'Sad? I'm not sad.' She swallowed painfully and tried to erase all emotion from her features, but her reflection didn't satisfy her. Smiling nervously, she tried to free herself from his hands. 'I'm going downstairs—Inger is waiting for me.'

He didn't let go of her. Still standing behind her, he grasped her arms, making it impossible for her to move away.

'What's the matter, Amy?' he asked.

'Nothing. Nothing's the matter.'

'Why are you trying to run away from me?'

'I am *not* trying to run away! I only want to go downstairs!'

'Are you afraid of me?' There was a glimmer of amusement in his eyes, sparking off more irritation in her.

'Don't be ridiculous!'

Almost imperceptibly his expression changed. 'I seem to remember times when you weren't so eager to get away from me.' His grip on her arms had tightened and it hurt. He wasn't going to let her go.

'These are different times,' she said coolly.

Silence filled the room, heavy, loaded with tension. Vic's jawline hardened and his face was dark and angry.

'Of course,' he said slowly, 'you're here on vacation.'

'Right.' And he'd better believe it.

'Well then....' He bent down, his lips caressing her neck, her ear. 'How about a little vacation romance? What's a vacation without a love affair?' His hands moved down slowly, stroking her breasts, and her breath caught in her throat and she thought her heart would stop. His caresses were infinitely sensuous, his lips were warm and soft against her skin as he kissed her. No caveman manners now. Still....

As if transfixed she stood there, her eyes closed, incapable of moving, feeling with horrifying clarity the awakening of her senses, feeling too, by instinct, the insincerity in him.

'What do you think?' he whispered in her ear. 'It'll be nice, you and I.'

'Please,' she said in a choked voice. 'Please let me go.'

He didn't comply. Instead he turned her around, held her very close so she felt every inch of his hard, strong body against her own, and she fought against the overwhelming need to give in to him, to relax in his arms. But he was playing with her, she knew. This was not the man she loved, not the man she wanted. Or was he? He kissed her with an urgency she couldn't fight, demanding response she couldn't withhold.

For months she had ached for his touch, feeling

drained of love and life after he'd left. Now she was back in his arms and fear and warning couldn't reach her. The long empty months fell away and memory betrayed her. She drifted away on clouds of sensuous feeling, knowing only this moment and the need for his love.

He released her suddenly, his face unsmiling, his eyes dark and shadowed.

'Well, that's more like it.' He turned and stalked out of the room.

The evening passed in a blur—faces, voices, laughter seemed to come from a long distance. All Amy was really aware of was Vic, his every movement, his laughter, and his eyes as he looked at her across the room, cool and indifferent. Fear was pressing down her spirits, fear that the man she had once known had gone for ever, that she would never find him back.

The conversation around her didn't penetrate her mind until suddenly a word struck her consciousness, stood out like lightning in the sky.

Tanya.

The name went through her like an electric shock. Her body tensed and her ears sharpened, taking in the rest of the conversation.

'*Tanya did that? Just the thing she'd do.*'

'*She's crazy.*'

Laughter.

'No.' It was Bunny speaking. '*Not crazy, just soft as butter. That girl has a heart of gold.*'

Amy closed her eyes, feeling the fear grow in her. *Tanya.* The girl's face appeared before her eyes—a pretty face. *A heart of gold.* Tanya—a *nice* girl. In the large blue eyes she had seen the sudden apprehension. She hadn't imagined it. And she hadn't imagined the towel, either.

'Are you seeing ghosts?'

It was Inger, collapsing next to her on the sofa.

'I still feel funny and tired. Does it take that long to get over jet-lag?' Amy was amazed by her own prompt and casual response.

'*Days* sometimes,' Inger said cheerfully. 'Listen, I've been wanting to ask you, what did Vic mean about "metamorphosis"? Did he do something secret or exciting before he came over here?'

Amy laughed. 'No, not really. What does he tell people here about himself?'

'Nothing, really. That he's an engineer, that he used to work in New York, that's all. But I've had the feeling there's a little more, I don't know what. He's not exactly like the rest of the volunteers. He's older of course, but....'

'Talking about me?' It was Vic, looming large overhead.

Inger laughed. 'Of course, who else? I'm trying to unravel the mysteries of your past.'

'Oh?' He raised one mocking eyebrow. 'Are you getting anywhere?'

Inger sighed, feigning disappointment. 'No. I don't think Amy is going to tell me anything.'

Vic looked at Amy, his face devoid of expression. 'Why don't you, Amy? Go ahead and tell her what kind of guy I was.'

CHAPTER THREE

SHE didn't like it, not one bit. Vic was after something, only she wasn't sure what.

What kind of guy?

He was different from all the other men she'd ever met. There was something intriguing, something very special about him. He was not impressed by his own accomplishments, seemed to think that having a lot of money was nice but not particularly important. He was interesting, warm, caring, and full of surprises. He loved his grandmother. He loved stray cats. He didn't laugh at her when she cried in a soupy movie. One day he brought her a clay pot with a parsley plant to put on her kitchen windowsill. He listened to her when she talked—about her worries, her joys, her kids in school. He took her out to expensive restaurants, but he preferred to eat at her place. She liked cooking for him—Italian dishes from old-world recipes her grandmother had given her. Vic insisted on doing the dishes. His own apartment sported a pushbutton dishwasher that lit up like a computer.

'What kind of guy?' Amy queried now. 'I don't know what you mean.'

'Yes, you do.' He was smiling now, but it didn't reach his eyes and it was only for Inger's benefit.

'Let's hear it,' said Inger. 'It sounds intriguing.' Her eyes gleamed like candles.

'Where do you want me to start?' Amy asked Vic. 'Your company, your apartment, the kind of life you had?'

'Whatever you prefer.'

Okay, if he wanted it, he could have it.

'He looked very different at home,' she began. 'I'd

never seen him in working clothes until I came here.
He used to wear suits or very expensive casual clothes.
You know where he lives now? Well, in New York he
had a penthouse apartment overlooking the city—
designer furniture, real art on the walls, a real movie
star place. He owned his own company, an engineering firm that he'd started himself. He drove a Jaguar.
He used to take me out to expensive restaurants and
Broadway plays.' She was aware of Vic, leaning against
the wall, observing her closely. Good. She turned
slightly away from him, pretending to ignore him completely.

'You should have seen the place,' she said to Inger.
'It was gorgeous!' She went on describing the furniture, the kitchen appliances, the bathroom fixtures,
speaking with an enthusiasm worthy of a sportscaster
covering an exciting football game. Listening to her
own voice, she was amazed and wondered how she did
it, how she could stand there and rave about leather
chairs and Mexican tiles as if they filled her life with
meaning.

Inger's eyes grew wider and wider and there was no
doubt she was impressed.

'Money, right?' she said at last.

'Lots of it.' Amy sighed. 'He got rid of the apartment and all the furniture. He even sold his company.'
She smiled regretfully. Too bad, her smile said, I liked
all the glitter, the gloss, the glamour.

Inger looked at Vic in awe. 'I knew there was something different about you. Money—it always shows,
doesn't it? Maybe I should call you sir. I'm not sure I
know how to behave around wealthy people. Had I
known I wouldn't have invited you to eat leg of lamb
and cabbage. . . .' Her tone was half serious, half joking.

Vic grinned at her, his old charming grin that Amy
knew so well. 'I wouldn't worry about it too much, if I
were you. I didn't bring my money with me as you

may have noticed, and I wouldn't miss your lamb for anything.'

Inger winked at Amy. 'He's nice, isn't he? So ordinary, despite all the wealth.'

In one reckless, impulsive moment, Amy knew the right reply. 'I think he's nice *because* of all that money,' she said, not looking at Vic.

Inger laughed out loud, but no reaction came from Vic. When she looked at him, she saw his eyes, dark and angry, his face grim. She smiled at him innocently.

'Are you angry?'

His expression changed as if she'd pushed a button. He smiled at her calmly, coolly.

'Not at all, not at all.'

It was late when they finally left the party. Amy wished she could have stayed with Gunnar and Inger, but there really was no choice, she'd have to go home with Vic. She felt as if she were diving head first into disaster. They were silent all the way home. There seemed to be strange vibrations emanating from Vic and instinctively she knew that she'd best be quiet. She knew she'd played a dumb game and she was sorry. What had made her act in such a ridiculous manner? Everything was getting to her and she hardly recognised herself.

'I hope you enjoyed yourself tonight,' said Vic as they entered the village. It was the first thing he'd said. His face remained in the dark and his voice was neutral.

'Oh, yes, I did. Everybody is very nice.'

'Not including me.' It was a statement, not a question.

Amy bit her lip. 'You seem so different.' Why did her voice wobble? She swallowed. 'I'm sorry.' She was saying sorry for all that seemed to be wrong, only she still didn't know how and why it was all wrong, or what to do about it.

Vic opened the door and they entered the house. 'Different? Well, you don't quite seem to be the girl I remember, either.' He groped for the pressure lamp and started pumping it up. 'That little performance with Inger tonight was quite a surprise.' He lit the lamp and a soft light spread through the room.

'What do you mean?' She knew perfectly well what he was talking about, but she wanted to hear him say it.

He stared at her for a moment, his mouth a thin line.

'*He's so nice because of all that money.*' He repeated her words with scornful emphasis.

'You asked for it!' she snapped.

'Oh? How's that?'

'You put me on the spot. What had you expected me to tell her? If you play silly games, so can I!' She turned and made for the door, but he took her arm.

'Sit down,' he ordered.

'No! It's late. I'm tired and I want to go to bed!'

'I want to talk to you.' He was holding on to her arm with iron determination, his face very close, his voice low.

'I don't see what there is to say,' she said belligerently.

'Well, *I* do. There's something I think you'd better know, so sit down.'

She had no choice, so she lowered herself into a chair. Vic remained standing, towering over her, looking down on her with eyes that suddenly seemed tired and weary.

'You may think that what I'm doing here is just a fling, something I'll tire of after the newness wears off. That's what my family and friends back home seem to think.' He sighed suddenly. 'Well, I have a surprise for you. I have no intention to go back to my former life style, Amy. That's gone and over with. You have to understand that. I can make better use of my abilities

in places where there's more need for them. I don't
give a damn about three-piece suits, fancy cars and
penthouse apartments. And if that's why you fell in
love with me, I can only repeat to you: Go home, girl.
There's nothing for you here.'

Amy could feel the colour drain from her face. 'You
don't think that I liked you because of that, do you?'
There was a sick feeling in the pit of her stomach. Had
he taken it seriously what she'd said to Inger? With
her hands clenched in her lap she watched his expression, feeling cold and miserable.

'You seemed to enjoy perfectly well all those things
that money can buy,' he said coolly.

Anger swelled in her throat and she was no longer
cold. 'And what's wrong with that? Just because I
liked being spoiled by you it doesn't mean it's all I
care about! What's money and luxury when there's
nothing else?'

There had been more, so much more, but she didn't
know how to put it into words. Beneath the glamour
of Vic's life there had been something else, something
very special that had attracted her to him. How could
she tell him about that now? He would laugh in her
face. Her anger ebbed away and sadness filled her.

'You think I'm ... I'm some kind of empty-headed
gold-digger....' She swallowed, trying desperately to
keep control over her emotions. 'I didn't come here to
chase your money, Vic. I don't need it and I never
have. As I told you, I'm here on vacation—nothing
more and nothing less.' By some miracle her voice was
calm and steady, the way she wanted it. There was no
use in getting angry or upset. It didn't matter any
more, it was too late.

Vic said nothing, just stood there, looking at her.
Amy wanted to stand up, but he was blocking her way.

'Please,' she said, 'I'd like to go to bed now.'

He reached for her hands and pulled her up. There
wasn't enough room between him and the chair, but he

didn't step aside, just held her there against him. She
tried to wriggle free of him, somehow, but he wrapped
his arms around her, holding her tighter yet, and she
was trapped. She closed her eyes, trying to block out
his nearness, but she could feel the pressure of his body
and there was no way she could keep herself from
trembling. He had to feel it too, she was sure. She
took a shaky breath.

'Please let me go.'

'Oh, my God, Amy,' Vic muttered in a strangled
voice, 'let's stop this nonsense.' He bent his head, his
mouth searching for her lips in hungry urgency.

Let's stop this nonsense. More than anything else she
wanted to do just that—forget the last few days that
held only anger and hurt. Go back to the way it was,
love him, be loved by him.

His kisses, warm and deep, took away all remnants
of apprehension and she let herself go, kissing him
back, not caring. She'd never had any resistance to the
magic of his touch, never could do anything but re-
spond to it with every part of her being. The warmth
of his body seemed to flow over into hers, giving her a
delicious sense of lightheadedness. Every inch of her
was reacting to the feel of him, wanting him, loving
him.

'I can feel your heart,' he whispered as he covered
her breast with his hand, and the look in his eyes stopped the breath in her throat. 'Amy, I want you.' His
voice was dark and deep with desire. 'I want to hold
you and touch you and feel you all over.'

No coherent thought entered her mind. Her pulse
throbbed wildly in her throat. She looked at him in
numb longing. Then, over his shoulder, something
blue caught her eye.

The towel. The towel that he'd left at Tanya's
house. An icy hand gripped her heart and she froze.

Vic's hand moved away from her breast and he
touched her face with tender fingers. 'What's wrong,

Amy?' he asked softly. 'There's nothing wrong in me wanting you, is there?'

Yes, there is! she thought fiercely. *Wanting me, or Tanya, whoever happens to be handy!* He hadn't wanted her to come, but now that she was here, he might as well make the best of it. Was that what he was thinking? She strained against him and the blinding pain in her heart was worse than anything she'd ever experienced.

'Amy? Are you afraid?' An incredulous look came into his face. 'I won't hurt you.'

'Let me go,' she said in a choked voice. 'Please let me go.'

He released her slightly, lifting her face. 'You're crying! Oh, Amy, I'm sorry. I don't mean to force you into anything you don't want.'

She turned her face away from him, hating him for his tenderness and concern, wishing she could believe in his sincerity. Was he like that with Tanya too? Was he just like that with any other woman? The thought seared through her heart. Did he think that if he'd be nice to her, she'd fall for him too? Probably the tactic had worked with other women, but she wasn't going to let him use her. Not like that.

'Amy,' he said quietly, 'can't we talk about it?' His hand stroked her back, but she remained unyielding under his touch, feeling cold and empty inside. Her eyes were glued to the towel draped over the back of a chair.

'Amy, answer me!'

She took a deep, shuddering breath, looking up at him with all the dignity she could muster, willing her voice to be steady.

'I don't want to talk about it.'

'Amy,' he said softly, 'have you never slept with a man before?'

The blood rushed to her cheeks. 'It's none of your business!' How did he dare! How did he dare ask her a question like that! She wanted to run, but there was no escape from his arms.

He regarded her silently, a half-smile curving his mouth, then he smoothed her hair, gently, slowly. 'Why are you so defensive? It's not a crime, you know, to be a virgin.'

'I should think not!'

'I suppose it must be quite an accomplishment, actually.'

He was right about that. She deserved a medal. Steven, Tony—Vic was the first man she'd ever wanted. And he had walked out on her.

'I didn't mean to frighten you, Amy. There's nothing to be scared about. Let's sit down and talk about it.'

'No! You're all wrong! I don't want to make love, but it's not what you think. You don't understand, you just don't understand!'

She wished desperately she could get away from him. Never before had she felt so trapped.

Vic was silent for a moment and she could feel his eyes on her, but she couldn't make herself look at him. Then he sighed. 'No, maybe I don't understand. Maybe I was wrong all along.' His voice was toneless. He released her, stepping back to let her go. 'Goodnight, Amy.'

Sunday dawned, promising nothing good. It was dark and rainy and the house was silent like a cave. Was Vic still in bed? Had he gone? Hoping not to encounter him, Amy went to the kitchen to see what there was to be had for breakfast. Coffee. Bread, but no way to toast it. Jam. Cheese. A continental breakfast—why not? With the food on a plate she returned to her room, which looked dreary like a cell. She sat on the bed, cross-legged, and ate her bread dropping crumbs on the sleeping bag. What's wrong with me?

she wondered as she leafed through a glossy magazine she'd brought from home. The ads had all the answers. Vitamins promised health, beauty, happiness. So did yogurt. Perfume would make him dream of you day and night. So would silk underwear.

There was an article on creative kissing, and another one on how to conduct an affair without getting emotionally involved. (Who'd want to?) What she needed was an article on how not to be involved when you were *not* having an affair.

She read the horoscope. It predicted exotic travel (this?) and rollicking good fun with the sensuous, amorous man of her dreams (how wrong could they be?). It offered the advice to give in to explosively erotic impulses when the moon moved into her sign of romance (not a chance!).

She tossed the magazine aside and found paper and pen. 'Dear Sue,' she wrote, 'I've just had my breakfast of stale bread and jam and instant coffee. I'm sitting in my room which has a marvellous vista of a mud hut village soaking in the rain. To keep me company there are spiders on the wall, big black ones. Vic says they're harmless and impossible to get rid of, so I count them as part of the furniture, which would give you the shivers as well. Romantic, isn't it? Still wish you could have come with me?'

Amy stopped, finished her coffee and sighed. Staring out the window, she wondered what else to write. Sue was going to want to know it all—into the details, which she had no intention of supplying. It was better to keep things light. She began to write again.

'Virile Victor, as you used to call him, is somewhere around, but I have no idea where. When I got off the plane, sparks were flying, but not the way you might imagine. What exactly happened, I don't know. I do know one thing—I would have been better off at home fantasising about a lost love and feeling sorry for myself. At least I would have Alan Alda on TV and a bag of chocolate chip cookies to console me. That's a lot more than I have here.

'As you may gather, things aren't working out and I don't think I'll be here long. Thanks for taking care of my place. I'll let you know when I'll get back.'

Amy signed her name, folded the paper and put it in her handbag. She'd have to find an envelope, stamps, a mailbox.

If anything, the letter had made her feel even more disconsolate. She couldn't write it all off as a mistake, a stupid idea, a flop. Her feelings were real and she knew it. She felt like a caged animal, trapped by her own love, defenceless, powerless. Was she not capable of doing anything but sit there thinking of Vic? Her whole body and mind seemed obsessed with him and the intensity of her feelings was frightening.

There were drawing materials in her suitcase, paper, paint, charcoal, and with another effort at distracting herself, she took them out and tried to concentrate on sketching the little group of mud huts she could see from her window. There were no people about and the rainy scene outside looked rather grey and dreary. It didn't do much to cheer her up and she didn't like the outcome of her efforts. Irritated, she crumpled up the paper and tossed it on the floor.

In college she had taken a lot of art courses. She was good, but not good enough to make her living by it. As a teenager she had dreamed of being an artist, of living in Paris, Rome, Amsterdam, making enough money to travel and live comfortably. She had romantic visions of herself sitting in Parisian bistros talking with other artists, of drinking wine on a moonlit Roman sidewalk restaurant, of painting on a rocky island off the coast of Greece. All of this in the company of a sensuous, romantic man, a tall blond, blue-eyed Swede—a poet, a painter.

Instead she had become a sensible schoolteacher,

fallen in love with a dark-haired, down-to-earth engineer whose work dealt with level lines, pounds of pressure per square inch, exact measurements, accurate calculations.

Vic liked her paintings, her charcoal sketches. He'd been sincere in his praise when he'd seen her work, although at first she had been reluctant to show them, afraid that he might have to pretend that he liked it for politeness' sake. His apartment had displayed several pieces of art, some of which Amy had recognised as quite valuable. There were also pieces by unknown artists, bought because he liked them.

More than once Vic had admired one of her paintings that hung on the wall in her apartment. A few weeks before he left he had his thirty-fourth birthday and she'd known that an appropriate present would be hard to come by. Spending a lot of money wouldn't have been right. It would have made him uncomfortable and he wouldn't have appreciated that kind of a gesture. It had occurred to her then that the painting he liked so much would be the perfect present, and she had been right. She had known as soon as she'd seen the expression of genuine pleasure that lit up his face when he opened the package.

'Thank you,' he had said. 'There's nothing I'd have liked better.'

Strangely, she felt uncomfortable. 'I don't mean to be pretentious, it's just that ... well, you said you liked it, otherwise I wouldn't have dreamed of giving it to you. ...'

He took her in his arms and silenced her with kisses that made her body tremble and her heart race.

'Yes,' he said, 'I like it. But it's doubly special because it's something of yourself you gave me.' Grey eyes held hers. 'Why would I think you pretentious? You're too modest. Your work is good and you should have a little more confidence in your own ability.'

Amy sighed. The paper in front of her was covered

with doodles, all she seemed capable of now. It was
cold and suddenly she shivered. Wrapping the sleeping
bag around her shoulders, she sat back down on the
bed. Was there any way they could recapture that feeling of love and trust and respect? But how could she
possibly ignore what she'd seen in Tanya's eyes? How
could she be sure he was sincere when he was holding
her in his arms when he'd been so angry at her at the
airport?

At lunch time there was a knock on her door. Vic.
Cord pants, a light grey sweater the colour of his eyes.
He looked big, formidable, alien. For a fleeting
moment a feeling of fear flew through her, then it
passed as she saw no sign of threat or anger in his face.
He was calm, self-possessed and utterly in control. Like
a marble statue, like a frozen lake.

Her own state of mind was anything but calm. It
was more like a turbulent ocean churning under a
tropical storm. She was trembling. Was it him? Was
it the cold?

'There's some lunch ready in the living room. Why
don't you join me in front of the fire? It's cold in
here.'

His calm, matter-of-fact attitude set her nerves on
edge.

'I'm not hungry, thank you.' Damn, she thought, I
sound just like a sulky child. Looking at Vic's face, it
apparently was exactly what he was thinking too. He
sighed like a weary father.

'Come on, Amy, don't be childish. There's no reason
for you to hide. Can't we be on friendly terms at least?'

Friendly terms? He must be joking! How was that
going to work? Then she shrugged and slid off the
bed. 'Okay, I'm coming.'

There was a tray of food on a small table in front of
the fire—hot vegetable soup and cheese sandwiches.
They ate in silence and the warmth of the food and
the fire spread through her. She hadn't realised how

chilled she'd been. Ice cube. Ice maiden. Was that what Vic thought she was?

'I didn't know it could be so cold here,' she said, breaking the silence.

'It's the rainy season and we're quite high up—five or six thousand feet, that's what does it. The rest of the year it's quite warm in the daytime, but it always cools off at night.' He put his soup bowl back on the tray. 'How about some coffee?'

'I'd like some. I'll go and make it.'

'It's my turn.'

She didn't argue; there was no point.

Vic stood up, gathered the dishes and left the room. When he came back, he handed her a cup, sat down and looked at the fire. 'I thought maybe we could talk about what you'd like to do and see while you're here,' he said. 'What did you have in mind?'

His question threw her off balance. For a moment she said nothing. Had she actually convinced him she was here on vacation only? She'd thrown him the ball. He'd caught it. Should it surprise her that he was throwing it back? Play it cool, she thought.

'I'm not sure. You have any suggestions?' Not bad.

His face was expressionless. 'Well, if you want to do the regular tourist routine, you're better off in Nairobi. There are all kinds of organised tours you could go on, camera safaris, sightseeing, whatever.'

Her mind produced images of zebra-striped tour buses, fat German ladies with bleached hair, gum-chewing, beer-bellied Californians, frail Japanese weighted down with photographic equipment. And all of them looking as if they were going on a survival expedition. How did she know? Where had she seen it? TV. Magazines. Somebody's vacation slides.

'I'm not really the tourist type,' she said, trying to keep unperturbed under his scrutinising gaze. 'I don't like tramping around in a group. I'd rather do something on my own.'

He nodded. 'I thought you would,' he said slowly, observing her closely for a moment. Then he stood up and began to poke around in the fire, sending sparks flying. 'If you want to see the real Kenya, you're better off right here. As you know, you're sitting right in the middle of it.'

She knew all right. All she had to do was look out the window and see the small huts, the bald-headed old women, the children playing in the mud puddles.

'Yes, I know, but....'

'If you stay here, you could come with me on some of my trips, and I'm sure Bunny would be delighted to give you a tour of the hospital.'

His sudden generosity and helpfulness stunned her. 'Are you asking me to stay here with you?'

He put the iron poker down, lowered himself in his chair and looked at her coolly. 'No, I'm not asking, I'm suggesting. Offering, if you like.'

Amy clenched her hands. Okay, point taken. She wouldn't get the wrong idea, if that worried him.

'It's very nice of you, but I don't want to impose on you.'

'You're not imposing. The house is big enough for an army.'

It could never be big enough for two people who didn't get along, she thought. Yet there was no other place for her to go, unless she wanted to go to Nairobi, play the tourist, or just go home and give up this hopeless expedition. Declare defeat. Come to terms with the fact that she had lost him to a new life and a new girl.

But I still love him, she thought miserably. I can't just give up without even trying. Trying what? She didn't know. All she knew was that if she left now it was over and as long as she stayed here something might happen. Like what? What she needed was a miracle, a fairy godmother, Aladdin's magic lamp.

'Is the thought of staying here too painful to consider?' There was mockery in his voice and his eyes were coolly amused.

'What do you mean by that?' she demanded.

'You should see your face.'

Anger suddenly took over. 'I wish you'd stop looking at me!'

Vic laughed. 'I like looking at you. I always did, you know.'

She had no reply to that. It had never bothered her before, because she had liked what was in his eyes then. But now everything was different.

His gaze didn't leave her face. 'Anyway, how about getting back to our discussion? Would you like to stay on here, or do you prefer to go to Nairobi?'

There was no way of avoiding his eyes. Some strange and powerful force held hers locked, as if she had no strength or will to look away. Her heart hammered wildly and her courage almost failed her.

'I'd like to stay,' she said.

The silence between them was alive with meaning, underlining her words, giving them a significance she hadn't intended. Vic said nothing, just looked at her, but whatever was in his thoughts, his eyes did not reveal. In a sudden frightening flash of memory Amy recalled what he had said the night of her arrival. Was he going to demand a pay-off for his hospitality? Was that why he wanted her to stay with him? If that were the case.... But her thoughts were interrupted when Vic stood up and once more began to rearrange the logs in the fireplace.

'Okay,' he said matter-of-factly, 'that's settled, then.'

Vic went to work the next day. The rain had stopped temporarily and it was warm and sunny. Amy gathered her courage and ventured into the village. People looked at her and children giggled as they followed her along the muddy paths, making her feel like the Pied Piper. She tried unsuccessfully to ignore them.

She couldn't shoo them away—she didn't know the words. All she could do was put up with them.

There was a row of small shops—*dukas*, Vic had called them—nothing more than a counter and a few shelves with soap and sugar and dried beans. One of the *dukas* was a little dairy with old-fashioned milk cans that looked scrubbed and shiny. There was a little butchery too, with a carcase hanging in a screened enclosure. A young girl came out, carrying a package wrapped in newspaper, a baby asleep on her back. Big black eyes looked at Amy curiously. Would she ever get used to being so conspicuously white and foreign? It was a strange sensation to be the one to stand out in a crowd, as if suddenly there was something very strange about her, as if she'd grown horns on her head or wings on her back—something.

From somewhere she heard children's voices, singing a song, or so it seemed. Following the sounds, Amy came upon a small shelter where a group of little ones were sitting on rough wooden benches in the shade of a thatched roof. A teenage girl stood in front of the group, directing the singing, and with a sudden excitement Amy realised it was a school, a nursery school. They could not see her from where she stood, and for more than twenty minutes she watched them with fascination.

There was nothing to play with in the school, no supplies of any kind. The children sat quietly on the straight benches, singing, and later counting—at least that was what it sounded like. After that the teacher let the children go and they ran out, laughing and shouting and suddenly all energy. They sat down on the ground where they played with the mud, empty tin cans, sticks and leaves.

Amy walked on to the edge of the village. The land stretched out in front of her, low sloping hills, and in the distance Mount Kenya, majestic, serene, with its snow-capped peak reaching up to the blue sky. On top lived Mungu, the god of traditional Kikuyu religion. Somebody had told her that. Vic? Gunnar? She didn't remember.

At home she took out her drawing materials and sat down at the dining table and tried to put down on paper what she'd seen in the village. This was not Rome or Paris or a Greek island. In some ways it was far more exotic, more romantic. In any case, it was a lot more interesting than New Jersey. Images of the little children under the thatched roof came back to her. Who'd have thought to find a nursery school in the midst of the African bush? Was there anything she could do to help? Maybe she could give them some paper and pencils, some simple toys like balls or building blocks, or maybe some picture books.

For a long time she sat absorbed in her work, making quick sketches in charcoal. When late in the afternoon Vic's Land Rover stopped in front of the house, the table was covered with a variety of village scenes—women standing in line at the water tap, children playing in the mud, a mother giving her baby a bath out in the open.

Vic strode into the room, pulling off his bush hat and throwing it into a chair. Mr Clean he was not, with his muddy boots and jeans. They should use him for a detergent commercial, Amy thought. *Nobody gets dirtier than this man. Would your brand clean these jeans?*

'Hi,' he said. He barely looked at her and Amy's heart shrank at his indifference. There was no such lack of feeling on her part. All she needed to do was lay eyes on him and her whole being sprang to life, wanting to go to him, touch him, hold him—dirt and all.

I still love him, she thought wildly.

She didn't understand it, not with her brain. She only knew that it was so, that despite the change in him, despite the hurt of knowing there was probably someone else, she still loved him. If only she could just shut it off! But love, she thought bitterly, was not a car engine or a coffee percolator.

'Hi,' she replied, looking away quickly, not wanting him to read her thoughts, but he wasn't even looking at her, and biting her lip she turned unseeing eyes back to her work. She'd have to stop feeling this miserable sense of rejection. If she wanted to stay she'd have to keep her emotions under control and play it cool.

Vic left the room, coming back half an hour later wearing clean clothes, and smelling of soap and shampoo. His hair was damp and clung to his head. He stood next to her and looked at the sketches, making no comments. He studied them for what seemed like a long time, picking up one drawing after another. Amy stared at his hand, hard and strong and brown. She wanted to reach out and touch it, feel the strength of his fingers.

'They're good,' he said at last. 'Really very good. Especially this one.' He pointed at the sketch of the children playing in the mud with empty cans and sticks.

'Thank you.' She didn't know what else to say.

'You could sell them in Nairobi, I'm sure.'

'Sell them? To whom?'

'Tourists love this type of thing. Touch them up a little, use some heavier paper and you're in business. The art shops will take them on commission.'

'You can't be serious,' she said a little breathlessly. 'I'm not that good, I mean....'

Vic smiled a funny smile. 'You're not in New York competing with top artists. You may never be a Rembrandt, but you do have talent. You know that, you've been told that. Your work has real charm, real honesty. Don't knock yourself, Amy.' Something of the old warmth was in his eyes, or maybe she imagined it. It lasted for a moment only, then his face returned to its calm, unemotional expression of before.

'Anyway, think about it.'

Amy did think about it—all that evening and the next day. It was an endless, empty day with Vic out to work and plenty of time to consider the question. To think that people might want to pay money for her work was exhilarating. It was probably the subject matter that appealed to them, she thought, as she examined the sketches that lay spread out in front of her. No, this wasn't New York, and being here worked to her advantage. What she could produce here she couldn't have done at home. What the tourists wanted they couldn't buy at home.

Sudden movement caught her eye and she looked up. A man was standing outside the window and fear shot through her when she saw the African staring at her, waving a *panga*. He was huge, his bare arms and torso masses of rippling muscles. Waving the sharp blade in the air, he looked infinitely dangerous.

Amy's heart pounded wildly and her eyes flew to the door. It was open, but it didn't have a lock, so closing it wouldn't do much good.

What did the man want? Horrifying possibilities raced through her mind and with shaking limbs she got up from her chair. Kariuki. Where was Kariuki? Taking a deep breath, she tried to steady herself. Don't get carried away, she told herself. He may have nothing violent in mind.

Nothing violent? Such as what? Borrowing a cup of sugar? Inviting her to tea? Peaceful people didn't wave machetes at others, and one more look at the fearsome-looking Goliath with the sharp tool in his hand did nothing to reassure her. A newspaper headline appeared before her mind's eye: NEW JERSEY GIRL MURDERED IN AFRICAN VILLAGE.

The man moved his dark bulk closer to the window, calling out at her, but she couldn't understand what he was saying and panic rose to her throat. What if he came in when he saw the door was open? The saner part of her kept telling her not to get hysterical, to go outside to find out what it was he wanted, but her rational mind couldn't overrule the terrible fear that immobilised her body. Her hands gripped the back of the chair, her knees shook uncontrollably. Still waving the *panga* in the air, the man kept repeating the words over and over, louder and louder.

She wanted to run, but her legs seemed stuck in cement and she couldn't move. *She could not move!* Her head was swimming, the room was swaying around her and she couldn't hold herself straight. I'm going to faint, she thought, horror-stricken. Dear God, I'm going to faint....

CHAPTER FOUR

As she started to feel herself slipping off into nothingness, she saw the Land Rover—and Vic, jumping out of it. The man turned away from the window.

Amy was still standing, holding on to the back of her chair, her whole body trembling. She sat down, slowly, putting her head down on her arms on the table and closing her eyes. When she opened them again the man had gone and Vic was standing in the doorway, his eyes fixed on her, totally perplexed.

'Good lord, what's the matter with you?' he demanded.

With trembling hands she smoothed her hair away from her face. 'I ... nothing. That man—what did he want?'

He frowned, looking puzzled. 'John? What did you think he wanted?'

'I don't know. He was shouting at me, waving that *panga*, and I thought....' A convulsive shiver ran through her. 'I thought....'

As he walked across the room, the expression on his face changed from surprise to amusement and he laughed out loud. 'Did you think he was going to attack you? Not only are you very impulsive, you have a very fertile imagination as well!'

And *he* had the sensitivity of a red brick, she thought as she took in his smiling mouth, the crinkly lines around his eyes. He was laughing at her, at the thoughts that had gone through her mind at the sight of the big man waving the sharp garden tool at her. Had her reaction really been so outrageous? Anger mingled with embarrassment, chasing away the weakness, the dizziness, and she straightened her back in defence.

'Funny, isn't it?' she said sarcastically. 'How could I possibly get such a crazy idea? I grow up with daily news stories about people being mugged and stabbed and killed and raped, but some stranger swings a twenty-inch blade in my face and I'm supposed to assume he has something peaceful in mind!' With a violent motion she shoved back her chair and stood up. 'How dare you laugh at me!'

His face straightened, became impassive. 'Sorry, I couldn't help myself,' he said in calm and serious tones. 'It did strike me as a little funny, though. This is a peaceful African village, not the New York City jungle full of junkies, pimps and drunks.'

'Well, pardon my ignorance!' she snapped caustically.

He grasped her shoulders. 'Now relax! You're over-reacting. I said I'm sorry!'

The feeling of his hands on her shoulders, warm and strong, suddenly drained her of anger. She shivered again, as if her body had to release the last remnants of fear and tension. Vic's nearness filled her with a deep longing to put her head against his shoulder, to warm herself in the comfort of his arms. But she could not, would not take that step, and staring at the buttons of his shirt, she tried to compose herself. They stood very still and the air was warm and heavy around them, full of some nameless emotion.

Then, taking a step backward, Vic let her go.

'John,' he said calmly, 'is a devoted husband and the father of four. He owns the butchery where I buy meat. He had no intention whatever to hurt you, believe me.'

Amy tossed her hair behind her shoulders and looked at him coolly. 'What was it that he wanted, if not to attack me?'

He sat down on a chair and started undoing the

laces of his workboots. 'John came to return the *panga*,' he said without looking at her. 'He'd borrowed it from Kariuki, but he wasn't here. All he wanted was for you to take it from him and give it to Kariuki.' His eyes were fixed on his boots and all Amy saw was his dark hair, tangled and in disarray from a day out in the open. Was he still laughing?

She had no way of telling.

They had dinner a while later and no further mention was made of the incident. They talked about Vic's work in the surrounding villages where he installed water systems he had first planned and designed.

He liked his work, Amy could tell by the sound of his voice alone. There was a rich quality of subdued enthusiasm, something she'd never heard at home. What he did here, he said, had an immediate impact on the lives of people. Just a simple pump was all it took. To think, he said, that he'd wasted his time designing bridges and tunnels and highways for a super-developed society where everybody took his work for granted and nobody knew his name. She laughed and said that bridges and tunnels and highways were important just the same. Of course, he said, but it was different. Working with village people who had a real need gave his work a sense of reality, added that human touch that his work at home had lacked. Did that make any sense to her? Of course it did, she said, and he smiled at her with a look in his eyes that made her heart lose its rhythm.

'Would you like to come with me tomorrow?' he asked. 'I'll show you what I'm talking about.'

'I'd love to.'

Again there was that smile, that look in his eyes. Oh, how she loved him!

The fork slipped from her fingers, clattering against the plate. The meal was finished, the discussion over.

Vic moved his chair back and stood up. 'Well, if you'll excuse me, I'll do some work.' Sitting down at

the large table at the far end of the room, he pro-
ceeded to study maps and blueprints. Something had
gone from the room. The atmosphere had lost its
warmth. Something had been happening while they
were talking, Amy knew. A delicate thread of understanding had linked them together—a touching of the
spirit.

Vic ignored her totally for the rest of the evening, as
if she weren't there at all, as if she were only a part of
the furniture. When she handed him a cup of coffee,
an absentminded 'thank you' was all she got. He
doesn't care that I'm here, she thought miserably. She
had a terrible urge to take his cup and pour the coffee
over his head—something, anything to make him
acknowledge her presence.

The crackling of the fire and the hissing of the two
pressure lamps were the only noises breaking the
silence. Sometimes Vic's papers rustled, or a donkey
brayed in the lonely darkness of the village. All he did
was work with what seemed to her an obsessive intensity. Was it really necessary to concentrate to the
extent where he couldn't even say an occasional word
to her?

For a while she found some distraction in writing a
letter to her grandfather, describing to him the village
and the people and telling him about her confronta-
tion with John. He would like to be here, she thought,
knowing how much he enjoyed doing things out of the
ordinary. His job as a reporter had taken him to many
strange places, and when Amy was younger he had
often taken her backpacking or fishing, telling her
wild and wonderful stories about his adventures. Now
those times with him were locked in her mind as precious memories.

The letter finished, she rose and started rearranging
the half-burned logs in the fireplace. It was then that
Vic finally got up from his chair and came to stand
beside her.

'I'll do that.'

Amy didn't move away, nor did her eyes leave the fire. 'It's all right, I know all about building and taking care of fires.' Her voice was flat and expressionless.

'You do? Okay, go ahead.' If possible, his voice sounded even flatter. He went back to his work and Amy felt like screaming.

Damn him, she thought. I'm going to bed.

Gathering paper and pen, she wished him goodnight.

He lifted his head briefly, but his face was empty of emotion and he didn't seem to really see her. 'Sleep well,' he said, and went back to work.

Sleep would not come. Why had he so blatantly ignored her all evening? What was it that she expected of him? Entertainment? She'd told him she'd come for a vacation, not for a romantic reunion. But it wasn't true, and all she really wanted was to get things right between them. But how? She might as well wish for Christmas to come in July, or for ice to melt at ten below zero.

Was Tanya a real threat, or was she imagining things? All she had to go on were the look in the girl's eyes, and the fact that Vic had left a towel at her house. But one plus one would always equal two and Christmas would always come in December.

He didn't want me to come here in the first place, she thought bleakly. He owes me nothing. There's no commitment and he never promised me anything.

She tossed around restlessly until finally she lay on her stomach, as she used to when she was a little girl, and closed her eyes. She counted sheep. At number two hundred and twenty-eight she gave up. Two hundred and twenty-eight sheep were altogether too many sheep to have floating around in your dreams. She went down the alphabet listing her favourite foods—anchovies, blackberries, chocolate eclairs, dill pickles, espresso coffee. F? Frog's legs? Yuk, no! She sighed. It wasn't working. Thinking of food wasn't going to make her sleepy; it was going to make her hungry. It *had* made her hungry. She groaned in frustration.

Her mind conjured up pictures of the little school, the children reciting numbers. How could she best help them? she wondered. Would the girl speak English? In what way should she approach her? She couldn't just butt in like some arrogant know-it-all.

She was drawing more pictures. Wide-eyed boys and girls in tattered clothes. Smiling faces, hands reaching out to her.

And then with a sudden sickening lurch of her heart she saw him again. He was back—the man with the *panga*. He entered the room, shouting, waving the *panga* at her.

Panic-stricken, she stared at him, her heart thundering in her ears. 'No!' she screamed. 'No, no!' She couldn't move. Her legs refused to function. He towered over her, huge, terrifying, his eyes glaring, his teeth gleaming white in a vicious grin. She felt icy-cold and shivered in sheer terror. In a desperate attempt to free herself she lurched forward with every ounce of strength she had in her, but nothing happened. He's going to kill me, she thought. He's going to kill me.

His free arm shot out and grabbed her around the shoulders, pulling her against him. With the other hand he raised the *panga*, holding it inches away from her throat. Then she screamed. Screamed and screamed in unbearable terror until no more breath would come. With everything in her she fought to be free, but his iron grip only tightened. Her whole body was immobilised by fear, and then, as if paralysed, her muscles relaxed and tension flowed from her body. I'm dying, she thought, but it didn't frighten her. There was no pain, only a peaceful feeling that seemed to fill her being with warmth and comfort. Then the knowledge slowly seeped through her senses that she wasn't dead.

She was awake.

She was awake, held by a pair of strong arms, her face against warm, bare skin, a low, strong heartbeat sounding in her ear. There was no need to look. She knew where she was and who was holding her.

A convulsive shudder shook her body and then relief flooded her—she was safe. Basking in the comfort of the arms that held her, she didn't move. Dead she was not, but this was surely heaven.

'You nearly gave me a heart attack,' Vic said softly.

'I did?' Her voice sounded muffled, her lips moving against his skin.

'You screamed bloody murder. I thought you were being killed.'

'So did I.'

There was a slight pause. He stroked her hair, smoothing away fears.

'John?'

'Yes.'

'Good God, he must have scared the living daylights out of you!'

'He did.' Again, helplessly, she shivered, and his arms tightened around her. She closed her eyes, feeling the warmth of her love for him satiate her being. She was aware of faint, undefinable vibrations between them and she knew she had to speak, say something, fill the silence with words.

'Maybe it's silly to be afraid,' she said, trying to sound normal, not to let him detect the tumultuous state of her feelings. 'I've seen horrible things about Africa on TV and....'

'Africa is a very big place.'

'Yes.'

I love you, she thought silently. *I love you.*

Vic trailed his fingers through her hair, absent-mindedly, or so it seemed. 'What you see on the news

are mostly political crimes.' His voice was calm and
without much inflection.

'Yes, I know,' she said against his chest.

Love me too, please love me too.

'You have to see these things in perspective. There
are fifty-odd different countries in Africa and the
majority are perfectly peaceful and as safe as your own
backyard.' He was speaking automatically, as if his
attention were directed somewhere else.

'I suppose so.'

I couldn't bear it if everything between us was over.

It was strange—she felt as if she were two different
people. One was talking in a perfectly rational manner,
the other was in total turmoil, with feelings of love and
desire and passion sweeping through her. Was Vic feeling the same way?

His fingers were stroking the nape of her neck, her
shoulders. 'You know,' he said, his voice betraying no
emotion, 'it's always the horror stories that make the
news. One dictator tyrannises or massacres innocent
people and the whole continent is looked upon as a
place of terror.'

'I never thought of it that way.'

This is crazy, she thought. *We're having a cool and
calm discussion as if we were sitting ten feet apart.*
But their closeness was undeniable, the atmosphere
filled with an unmistakable tension. Amy stirred in his
arms and her eyes caught the light of the candle he had
lit. Their shadows, strangely distorted, swept across the
walls and ceiling.

He bent his head, but only a little. 'Are you feeling
better now?' he said in her ear. There was a strange
note in his voice. Was it concern? Tenderness? Or just
sleepiness? Maybe he wanted to get back to bed, back
to his own room.

'Yes,' she murmured.

Don't leave me, she pleaded silently. *Stay with me.*

Minutes seemed to pass. They didn't speak. Their

bodies touched, but they didn't move. An element of expectation seemed to fill the room.

Kiss me, Amy begged wordlessly. *Please kiss me.*

But Vic's body remained perfectly still against hers, and only his rapid heartbeat and his irregular breathing betrayed that inside that silent rock of comfort he was trying to be, other feelings stirred. He wants me, she thought with tremulous elation, he wants me, I know.

Her heart pounded wildly and her blood raced with the fear of denial as she lifted her face and searched for his mouth, touching it with her own. It was as if an electric current passed through his body and she felt him tremble against her.

'Amy....' It came out on a sigh and she felt his breath brushing her lips. His mouth closed over hers and he began to kiss her, slowly, deeply, as he gently pushed her back on to the pillow. He stretched out, leaning over her, and in the far recesses of her conscious mind warning struggled briefly, but nothing could overpower the flood of emotion that washed over her. The ethereal sweetness of this moment was the only reality, the love flowing between them the only truth.

His hands caressed her quivering body, his breath warm on her cheek. Amy was incapable of reply, her senses leaving her empty of thought and reasoning. And then they were in each other's arms and nothing had ever been more sensuous than the feeling of Vic's warm, bare skin against her own, feeling all of him touching the full length of her body, making her come alive with desire—desire that seemed to flow from the centre of her being, released by a love that was real and true and undeniable. And it was good and right, and she knew it was so—a feeling beyond thought, beyond reason.

His hands moved down her body in tender exploration, and slow lingering kisses warmed her breasts. Mute with longing, she surrendered to the intimacy of his touch while tremors of strange, exhilarating excitement ran through her.

'Vic,' she breathed, 'oh, Vic....' She wanted to cry, she wanted to laugh—she didn't know why. She wanted him to go on and on and on and never stop.

'Amy....' He held her against him, tight with fierce urgency, his body trembling with his need for her. Then suddenly, with agonising effort, he tore himself away from her. Leaning on one elbow, he looked down on her, his eyes searching her face with a pleading intensity. He was breathing hard, his chest rising and falling rapidly, and she reached out and touched it, feeling the dark hair curling around her fingers, and she didn't want to speak now, only give in to the longing and the yearning that had taken possession of her body.

'Amy,' he said unsteadily, 'are you sure?' Gently seductive, his hand trailed down her hip, her leg, moved up again and came to rest on her thigh. She closed her eyes.

'Yes,' she whispered. 'Oh, yes!' Her voice sounded strange in her own ears—husky, dark. She pulled him down, feeling the warm, heavy weight of him, and she trembled with strange delight. She wanted him closer, closer, closer.... She wanted to be one with him. 'Please,' she whispered. 'Please!'

'Amy, there's something I want to tell you. I....'

A sudden loud knocking on the door thundered through her senses and she froze. *No!* Amy thought fiercely. *No! No!* Vic's body went rigid and he swore softly.

'*Bwana!*' It was Kariuki's voice, calling out in agitated tones.

'Damn!' Vic whispered fiercely. Then, in a louder voice, he answered Kariuki in Swahili. As he went to raise himself off the bed, Amy tightened her arms around him in desperate urgency, pulling him back against her in helpless desire.

'Don't go, Vic. Please don't leave me now ... not now.'

He groaned. 'I have to. Kariuki's wife has gone into labour. I promised him I'd take them to the clinic when the time came.' He wrenched himself away from her and strode towards the door.

Her mouth dry, her throat aching, Amy watched him miserably. Why, oh, why did it have to happen just now?

'Vic, I....'

He turned to face her. 'It's all right, Amy. It's probably just as well.' He sounded very tired.

'I don't know what you mean,' she said.

He came back to the bed and regarded her silently for a moment.

'Yes, you do,' he said at last. 'It wouldn't have solved anything, would it?'

There were tears behind her eyes and her throat ached with the effort not to cry. She didn't answer, but turned her face to the wall, away from him.

Vic bent down and kissed her cheek. 'Go to sleep, Amy. I'll see you in the morning.'

It took all her strength not to put her arms around his neck and pull him close again, to ask him to come back to her when he returned from the clinic, but she knew he would not.

Pressing back tears, she swallowed painfully. Vic walked to the door and she turned to watch him go. He didn't look back when he opened the door.

'Goodnight, Amy.'

He was gone. There were voices coming from outside, then the starting up of the Land Rover. Amy listened to the noise until it had diminished to a soft humming and finally disappeared in the night. Burying her face in the pillow, she cried out the pain and

the longing, feeling her fears and doubts returning
with increased intensity.

'*It's just as well,*' he had said, and maybe he was
right. She loved him, but she didn't want to share him
—not with Tanya, not with anyone. He had said something else, right before Kariuki had knocked on the
door. '*There's something I want to tell you.*' But he
hadn't said what it was. What could it have been? But
she couldn't think straight, and she didn't even want
to think, only sleep and forget everything—at least for
a while.

Finally, her tears spent, she lay limp and dry-eyed
waiting for sleep to come, but when Vic returned half
an hour later she was still awake. Her heart pounding,
she listened to his approaching footsteps, but they
didn't halt in front of her door.

It was a glorious morning, cool and sunny. But
glorious could in no way describe the way Amy felt,
physically or mentally. Having lain awake for hours,
she finally decided to get up. The sun bathed her room
in light, taunting her with its cheerfulness. Not bother-
ing to unzip the sleeping bag, she wrestled out of it,
kicking at it quite inelegantly. Damn, damn, she
thought, I feel like a rotten potato.

When she entered the living room Vic was sitting at
the table, drinking coffee.

'You look like hell,' he said with uncommon lack of
tact.

'So do you,' she shot back.

His lips quirked into a faint smile. 'It wasn't what
you call a restful night.'

'No.'

He could say that again. Amy buttered a piece of
bread with great care, spreading the butter evenly
from side to side with the precision and the concentration worthy of a brain surgeon. Another slice of bread

magically appeared on her plate and when she looked up her eyes met Vic's amused face.

'Why don't you do mine? You're doing such a beautiful job....'

'Okay.' She took a scoop of butter, flattened it on the bread with one sloppy slap of the knife and handed it back to him.

'I'm lousy at command performances,' she said sweetly.

'You could have fooled me.' He eyed the bread disapprovingly. 'You know what it feels like to sink your teeth into half an inch of greasy butter?'

'I try not to think about it.' She smiled. 'I wish you luck.'

'Wholeheartedly, I can tell.'

Kariuki came in with scrambled eggs on a plate, and a beaming smile on his face. What did *he* have to smile about? Oh, yes....

'How's his wife?' Amy asked after he had left.

'She's fine. She had the baby at five this morning— a girl.'

'Didn't he stay with her?'

'Sure. He walked back; it's not far.'

A thought occurred to her. 'What's he going to think?'

'About last night?' Vic shrugged. 'The obvious, and I don't give a damn. He probably didn't expect anything else. He sure knew where to find me.'

His indifference bothered her, only she couldn't quite say why. He was watching her over the edge of his coffee cup.

'Anyway, I'm sorry it happened,' he said, 'but let's not let it ruin the rest of the day.'

Now what was that supposed to mean? Was he sorry that Kariuki had interrupted them? Or was he sorry he had come to her room in the first place? Amy's heart shrank at the thought. Memory flashed by her—his mouth, his hands. . . .

'Vic?' Her heart hammered wildly, suddenly. 'Last night you were going to say something, just as Kariuki knocked on the door. What. . . .'

'Forget it,' he said shortly.

'Can't you tell me, please?'

He picked up the coffee pot, his face a blank. 'More coffee?'

He wasn't going to answer her, that was clear. She sighed. 'Yes, please. I'll need all the help I can get to stay awake for the rest of the day.'

He searched her face. 'Are you up to coming with me this morning? Or would you rather wait and do it another time?'

She shook her head. 'No, I'd like to come now. I'll be all right.' The last thing she wanted or needed was to hang around in an empty house all day, alone with thoughts that most certainly would never get an Academy Award for comedy.

Amy enjoyed the ride in the Land Rover, feeling the fresh, crisp morning air blow in her face, seeing the unfamiliar countryside. In most places the red soil of the dirt roads was still wet from the rains which kept the dust from flying around. Lush green hills alternated with stretches of flat land where cows grazed and Thompson gazelles leaped off in nervous flight at the approach of the Land Rover. They seemed to fly through the air, their feet barely touching the ground, their legs stretched out in an almost horizontal line.

Excitement surged through her. Glorious Africa all around, wide-open spaces, wildlife, sunshine. It's like a movie, she thought, and I'm in it. Look at me, riding in a Land Rover through this wild and free world— like Virginia McKenna in *Born Free!* She smiled a little at the idea and glanced at Vic, thinking that he looked as if he belonged in a movie—tough and brown and handsome. Her eyes went back to the countryside.

'What about those herds of elephants you see on movies and in pictures?' she asked. 'Will we see some of those?'

He shook his head. 'Probably not. They're out in the forest in the daytime. In the game parks you find the big herds out in the open, and a lot of other big game too—rhinos, buffaloes.' He pushed his bush hat back a little, smiled. 'Here you mostly see different kinds of buck, Tommies, some giraffes and ostriches.'

'I'd love to go on safari,' Amy said dreamily. 'It must be really something to see all those big beasts roaming around freely. I've only seen them in the zoo, locked away behind bars.'

He nodded, eyes on the road. 'You can go to Nairobi and take a package tour before you leave.' His voice was perfectly normal with no particular inflection.

But I don't want to go home! she thought. *I want to stay here with you!*

'I'll probably do that,' she said tonelessly.

Vic looked up at the sky. 'No rain today, it looks like. It's getting hot already.' With one hand on the steering wheel, he began shouldering his way out of his denim jacket. 'Give me a hand with this, will you, please?'

She did. He rolled up his shirt sleeves, requesting no assistance, and Amy stared at his strong, muscled arms, which were deeply tanned and covered with dark hair. These were the arms that had held her last night, but now she didn't even dare touch him.

In the village they were greeted by several men, two of whom crawled into the back of the Land Rover, and they drove a short distance out of the village to a small stream where the pump had been installed. Vic checked the mechanism, explaining to Amy how it worked. The water was piped into the centre of the village, he said, and it saved the women the time-consuming task of walking all the way to the stream and carrying the heavy *debes* back to the village.

'*Debes?* Those cans I see them carry around?' Amy asked.

Vic nodded. 'They used to have kerosene in them.'

He talked to the men at some length, apparently making sure they understood the workings of the pump. Amy thought again of bridges and tunnels, saw the glow in his eyes, saw the people standing around him. He likes this, she thought. I love him. Her mind produced the thought automatically. It was there, it would always be there. I wouldn't care if he wanted to design mousetraps, she thought. I wouldn't care if I had to live here for the rest of my life.

She watched him, the tall strength of him, the free and easy movements of his body, noticing how his working clothes seemed to accentuate his masculinity, and a heady warmth flowed through her, making her feel curiously weak.

Just then he looked her way and she smiled at him coolly, hoping he hadn't noticed what she knew must have been visible on her face. That was all she needed—have him catch her looking at him like some lovesick teenager staring at Robert Redford.

His face revealed nothing. He swung himself behind the steering wheel and they all climbed in the Land Rover and drove back to the village. Vic showed her the tap and she watched the women as they stood in line with their *debes.*

'Come on.' Vic took her arm and manoeuvred her away from the hordes of curious children that had surrounded them as soon as they'd entered the village. 'We've been invited to have some *chai.*'

They entered a small shack that apparently was a kind of café, and they were served tea in water glasses. It was brewed with milk and heavily sugared and had a character all its own. While Vic talked some more with the men who had accompanied them Amy watched two other customers who were playing what seemed to be Chinese Checkers. The board was a piece of cardboard and bottle caps served as checkers. A little bit of imagination could go a long way, Amy thought. A little bit of imagination had won the Greeks the city of Troy.

There were ways she could do things in the little school in Vic's village. Simple toys could be made from boxes, empty cans, and pieces of wood. Suddenly her mind was spinning with ideas and she was absorbed in thought when Vic's hand waving in front of her eyes pulled her back to reality.

'You were far, far away,' he commented, pulling her up from the bench and out of the shack.

Not so far, she thought, not so far at all.

The next village was much the same—laughing children, another pump, barefooted women filling *debes* at the tap.

They had lunch at the village butchery. Vic ordered—Amy didn't know what. She was tired, suddenly, her eyes burning from sun and dust. Sitting down at the rough wooden bench, she closed her eyes.

'Tired?' he asked.

'A bit. It's hot.'

'Don't sit in the sun.'

She opened her eyes. There was some shade on the other side of the wooden table, next to him. She'd have to sit close—too close.

'It's all right,' she shrugged.

'Don't be ridiculous,' he said flatly. 'Come on over here or I'll drag you.'

There was no fight in her. She sat down next to him, legs and arms almost touching.

'You want a beer? A Coke?'

'They have *Coke* here?' she queried.

'Certainly. Where did you think we were? The end of the world?'

'Couldn't be far from it.'

'You haven't seen anything yet,' he assured her.

The Coke wasn't cold, but at least it was wet. No refrigerators, no electricity—it was a different world. Amy viewed the surroundings. Thatched roofed mud huts, half-naked children, women carrying firewood on bent backs, like beasts of burden.

'I thought African women carried things on their heads,' she said.

'Most of them do, but not the Kikuyu women.'

'Looks very uncomfortable.'

'They're not doing it for fun.' Vic was playing with his keys while he drank his beer.

Inside the *duka* a slaughtered animal was hanging on a hook from the ceiling. It was surrounded by a screened frame. It couldn't be a cow—it was too small. Outside a man was roasting chunks of meat on a charcoal fire.

'Is that for us?' Amy asked.

'Yes.' Vic took off his sunglasses, looked at her. 'Are you hungry?'

She nodded. 'What is it?'

'Goat meat.'

'*Goat meat?*'

'Truly.' His eyes laughed at her. 'Here it comes.'

A wooden board was placed in front of them and Amy regarded the meat with suspicion.

'What does it taste like?' she asked.

'Like goat meat.'

'Funny. Very funny!'

There was a dull, flat feeling inside her. She was talking automatically without much thought or emotion, as if her brain was nothing more than a batch of lumpy mashed potatoes. Was it fatigue? The midday heat? The onset of depression?

'Here's how you do it.' He picked up a piece of meat with his fingers and dipped it in a little pile of salt that was on the board. 'Now you eat it.' He put it in his mouth.

'I've never had goat meat,' said Amy, wondering if

her stomach would stand up to the experience.

'You didn't come all the way over here to eat hamburgers, did you?' His eyes mocked her.

She shrugged, didn't answer.

'Be adventurous. Try it. You may be surprised and like it.' Obviously, *he* did. He ate another piece with relish. 'It won't kill you, you know,' he said, derision still in his eyes.

Damn him, she thought. She picked up a piece of meat, dipped it in the salt and ate it.

It was good, really very good.

'You want another Coke?' asked Vic.

'Yes, please.' She was thirsty. The sun glared over the village. From a short distance a small group of children were watching them eat.

'Do you ever get used to people staring at you?' she asked.

He shrugged. 'To some extent. You learn to ignore it.'

Like he was learning to ignore her. His arm kept touching hers as he reached out for more meat, but their closeness seemed to have no effect on him at all and his face never registered any reaction. I might as well be a stone wall, she thought.

'Have you thought about selling your pictures?' he asked.

Amy hesitated. 'Do you really think they'd sell?'

'I told you so.' He fished some money out of his pocket and paid for the meal. Picking up his keys, he got up from the bench. 'I want to go into Nyeri and pick up my mail. There's a store there where you may find some supplies.'

Amy followed him to the Land Rover. Maybe she could find something for the school there, too. Suddenly some measure of enthusiasm flared through her, and she told Vic about the little school and what she had seen.

'It's pathetic! There's nothing to play with, no toys

or games or anything. Just a roof with benches underneath. I want to buy them some paper and pencils and crayons, some simple toys....'

'Here you go again, diving off the deep end. Don't you ever learn?' He was frowning and didn't look pleased.

His reaction took her by surprise, and she stared at him. 'All I want to do is buy them some paper and....'

'Calm down and use your head. You'll do no such thing.'

Surprise changed into anger. 'Why not? I want to!'

'Why don't you give it some thought before diving in head first?' Vic leaned against the Land Rover, regarding her with a mingling of impatience and frustration.

'Why don't you stop treating me like a child!'

'Because you behave like one, dammit!' His jaw tightened and he shoved his hands into his jeans' pockets with ill-concealed irritation. 'First tell me this: What happens when the paper runs out?'

Amy shrugged. 'I'll buy them some more.'

He sighed. 'And what if you're not here?'

'I ... I don't know. I haven't thought about that yet.'

'Right, that's what I thought. Well, let me tell you. You're picking up right where the colonialists left off— oh, with all sincere motives, I know. But what you're doing is creating a need where none was before, resulting in one more dependency. Self-sufficiency is what development is all about, and you're not helping by handing out gifts and favours in that way.' He opened the car door and got in behind the wheel.

A sinking feeling of disappointment settled inside her. Undoubtedly he was right. She had never thought in those terms. Surely there was something she could do, though, something that didn't require the layout of money. She sat down in the car and sighed.

'But I want to do something. I want to help. I'm a

teacher and my experience should be worth something!'

Vic started the engine. 'Maybe. Maybe not,' he said dryly.

'Well, it should! I could help this girl, give her some ideas, show her how to do some things....'

'Amy, listen to me. Did it ever occur to you that she might not want your help? People have their pride, you know. Everyone involved may be perfectly happy with the way she runs the place. You're a stranger and this girl may resent your interference. You don't just step in and take over.'

'I wasn't going to do that!'

'It sounded like it.'

'Well, I wasn't! I'm not altogether stupid!' She turned her face away, biting her lip. She felt inexperienced, inept. The whole situation was so much more complicated than she had anticipated.

Vic manoeuvred the Land Rover out of the village on to the dirt road. Children waved. The sun still glared. Amy felt tired again.

'Did the girl ask you for your help?' he asked after a pause.

'No.'

'Let me give you some advice. Wait until she asks you. You won't get anywhere if she doesn't want you in her school.'

She didn't answer, didn't look at him.

'Amy?' The anger had left his voice. She glanced at him quickly.

'Yes?'

'I don't mean to patronise you. I know you're a good teacher and you mean well, but it's never as simple as it looks.'

You're right, Daddy, I'm sorry, Daddy, I won't do it again, Daddy. Amy wanted to say it out loud, but didn't. She shrugged instead, her eyes fixed on the road. 'It doesn't matter. It was just an idea. No big deal.'

Nothing matters, she thought with a sense of defeat. Why do I even try?

They drove back to Nyeri. They talked—a word here, a word there, empty conversation that blew away on the breeze across the plains. Now and then they saw some game—ostriches, antelopes and more Tommies. The lack of sleep the night before had dulled her senses and her body felt numb with fatigue. The uneven dirt roads didn't make for a relaxing ride and she felt like a rubber dummy bouncing around in her seat. She was relieved when they finally reached town.

Vic pointed out the post office, the book store, the grocery store, and Amy took some letters from her bag. 'Would you mail these for me when you're at the post office?' she asked.

'Sure.' He took the letters from her. 'Meet me at the grocery store when you're done,' he said. 'I need a few things.'

'Okay, I'll see you in a little while.'

He pocketed his keys and they both got out of the Land Rover. Amy watched him go. He was taller than anyone else in the street, walking with long, even strides. Head high, shoulders straight, he moved with the ease of a man who knew himself, a man who didn't give a damn what the world thought about him. He disappeared inside the post office and Amy turned, walking the opposite way.

It didn't take her long to find what she wanted and she deposited her purchases in the Land Rover before she entered the grocery store.

At first she didn't see Vic, then she heard him laugh, a good, hearty laugh, and she would have recognised the warm, deep sound of it in the middle of a crowd. She walked farther down the aisle and then she saw him. She stopped dead in her tracks, her heart lurched, and her stomach felt as if it was full of wet cement.

He was talking to Tanya.

So? her cool calm brain said; he also talks to the butcher, the baker, the candlestick maker. It means *nothing*.

Still, the sight of the two of them together was enough to make fear and suspicion take over her body and have a heyday. Her heart thumped, her knees trembled, her throat thickened. Oh, God, she thought helplessly, this is too ridiculous for words. It's ludicrous, it's absurd.

So why wasn't she laughing? Why did she have this terrible sense of foreboding every time she thought about Tanya or set eyes on her? Was it just sick jealousy founded on nothing but suspicions blown out of all proportion by an over-active imagination? Or was it a more subtle kind of female intuition?

As if transfixed, she stood in the aisle, her eyes glued to the girl's slender form. A good figure, a nice face, glossy hair. But in no way did she look like any kind of femme fatale. She was just a pretty girl, a girl with a 'heart of gold.' A girl who liked peanut butter sandwiches, rabbits, and walking in the rain.

She was laughing up at Vic, her blue eyes bright and shining, her face radiant. It took no intuition, no great sensitivity to interpret the girl's expression.

Tanya was in love with Vic.

CHAPTER FIVE

VIC's back was turned towards her and Amy couldn't see his face. She didn't want to. Unseeingly she scanned the shelves—bottles and cans and boxes in bright colours all blurring together. Soap, detergent, shampoo, toothpaste. Clenching her jaws, she fixed her eyes on a blue box of laundry detergent, forcing herself to read the printing, to calm herself down, but it was no use. Her gaze settled again on the two at the end of the store, seeing Tanya's happy face, the bright sparkle in the blue eyes. She was saying goodbye and started to leave. 'See you next Thursday!' she called over her shoulder as she swung down the aisle towards the door.

A force outside herself took hold of Amy's legs, moved her into another aisle and out of the store ahead of Tanya. She walked down the street, not knowing where she was going, aware only of the words that kept repeating themselves in her mind. 'See you next Thursday, see you next Thursday....'

After a while she suddenly realised she'd gone a long way and it was time to turn back. Across the street, a white figure caught her eyes. It was Bunny in uniform, waving at her and crossing the street to meet her.

'Amy! I thought it was you!'

'Hi. Are you coming from the hospital?'

Bunny nodded. 'Is Vic in town?'

'Yes. He's at the grocery store. I'm sort of scouting around.' Amy felt self-conscious, but didn't know why she should. Bunny's eyes flicked over her, then she smiled.

'Looks like you went on safari with him today.'

Amy grimaced as she surveyed her dusty jeans and

shirt. 'It shows, doesn't it?'

'Sure. Makes you look like one of us. Where did you go? Did you have a good time?'

Talking with Bunny was easy, requiring a lot of listening and not much talking, which was just fine with Amy. Bunny was worthy of her name. Her conversation hopped and bounced through a variety of subjects in a matter of minutes—the trials and tribulations of being a nurse, the miseries of living alone now that Cindy had left, the joys of eating the whole box of cookies her mother had sent.

'She thinks I'm perishing in the middle of darkest Africa, with nothing to eat but monkey stew and dried leaves. She read that in a book, she says. I don't fool her, she says. I told her that I'm eating better here than at home. I'm eating *steak*, I told her. Kenya *exports* meat—beef, pork, poultry—*respectable* stuff. But she doesn't believe me.'

Bunny sighed, stopped in the middle of the street and put her hands on her lips. 'Look at this! I've gained ten pounds since I got here!'

'Have you ever had goat?' Amy asked, remembering her culinary adventure of a few hours before.

'Oh, yes, lots of times. It's good, I love it, but you'd better believe I never told my mother about it.'

They wound their way through the crowded street and Bunny followed Amy into the store where they found Vic paying for his purchases.

He glanced at Amy. 'There you are,' he said, putting his change back into his pocket. 'I wondered what had happened to you.'

Apparently he didn't expect an answer. He picked up the box of groceries and turned to Bunny. 'Hi. How are you doing? Enjoy having the whole place to yourself?'

Bunny pulled a face. 'No, not really. I'm not much of a loner. I don't like living by myself, I need someone to push around.'

He grinned. 'There's a whole bunch of lonely volunteers out in the bush. I'm sure they'd love to keep you company.'

Bunny wrinkled her nose. 'I'm not *that* lonely! I'm very choosy, you know. I'm holding out for someone classy and rich. And handsome, of course.' She paused, frowning, as if she were making sure she hadn't left out other considerations. 'I'm aiming for an easy life, a big house with a sauna and a swimming pool, ski vacations and travel around the world.' She gave them a wide smile and Amy couldn't help laughing.

'How about a doctor?'

'Never!' Bunny's face registered great distaste. 'I don't like doctors!'

'But you're a nurse!'

'Exactly.' There was a wealth of meaning in her voice.

'Anyway,' said Vic, 'ordinary doctors don't have the money or the time to travel around the world at their leisure. Unless of course you catch yourself a plastic surgeon from California, the type that does cosmetic surgery on rich ladies.'

Bunny didn't reply—the menace in her expression was all-explanatory.

Vic's mouth twitched and his eyes were gleaming with laughter. He shifted the box in his arms. 'Come on, Amy. I think we'd better leave.'

A few days went by and Amy worked on her sketches and wandered through the village several times to get more ideas. The children still followed her, but she didn't really mind any more. They wanted to touch her—her arms and her hair, curious as to how they would feel. People greeted her with smiles and once she saw John in front of his *duka*, playing with his children. He was laughing and joking with them and he looked like a happy father anywhere—friendly, harmless. The old women with their bald heads and their stringy earlobes didn't seem so threatening any more.

Vic was a friendly stranger, making no efforts to come closer to her. He talked about Kenya, about his work, treating her in every respect as if she were there for a vacation only, as if indeed they were only casual friends. Did he not feel the undercurrents that were always there when they were alone together? Was she the only one who was aware of the vibrations between them?

To Amy the evenings were almost unbearable. He worked furiously every night, paying little attention to her most of the time. She would stare at his back, feeling miserable and alone, wanting only to be held by him again. But he never once touched her and she didn't know how to resolve her fears and doubts. She could only wait, wait.

Wambui, Kariuki's wife, had come back from the clinic and Vic took Amy to see the mother and baby late one afternoon. The smoky interior of the hut made Amy cough and it took a minute before her eyes were used to the dimness. Wambui was sitting on a straight-backed chair, the baby, wrapped in a green towel, in her lap.

Impulsively Amy reached out. 'May I hold her, please?'

The baby was beautiful. Her eyes were tightly shut and didn't open when Amy picked her up, but the tiny mouth puckered up and made sucking motions.

'She has so much hair!' she exclaimed in amazement, stroking the thick mass of curls on the baby's head.

'I've never seen an African baby without hair,' Vic said, observing her with both hands in his pockets.

'She's lovely,' Amy handed the baby back to Wambui, who began to talk to her in rapid Swahili. Amy looked at Vic for help and saw him grinning widely.

'What's so funny?' she asked.

'She says she hopes you'll have a baby soon, too.'

Amy's eyes widened. 'Me?' He had to be kidding.

'Sure,' he said casually. 'Don't you like babies?'

'Don't be ridiculous!'

'There's nothing ridiculous about getting pregnant.'
He was dead serious now, his grey eyes fixed on her
intently. 'It's very easy, as a matter of fact. I hope you
realise that.'

She could feel her face grow warm with colour, but
she didn't avert her eyes.

'I know. I'm neither ignorant nor stupid.'

'I'm glad to hear it.' He turned back to Wambui who
was talking again. Later, they walked back to the house
in silence while dusk settled over the village. The huts,
the *dukas*, the banana plants all blended together and
became indistinguishable shapes in the early darkness.

Another quiet evening. They had dinner. Coffee.
Silence. Vic worked for a while, then joined Amy near
the fire where she sat reading a book, some dreadful
tale about death and disaster.

Vic had to go to Nairobi the next day. He had an
appointment with someone in the Ministry of Works,
he said. Would she like to come with him and have a
look around? Yes, she said, she would.

Silence again.

'I hate this book,' she said.

'Throw it in the fire.'

She stared at him. 'Throw it in the fire?' she repeated.

'It's trash. It deserves to be burned. It's the most
morbid stuff I've ever read. I didn't even finish it.' He
took the book from her fingers, threw it in the fire and
grinned with satisfaction as the flames curled the
pages.

Amy smiled. 'Now I'll never find out what happened to Yellow Peter!'

'He gets assassinated, like the rest of them. Decapitated, to be more specific. You want the gory details?'

'No, thanks.'

'Good. I didn't read that far, but I thought that in a pinch I could make them up.'

Amy laughed, watching the book shrivel away in the flames.

'Sometimes,' said Vic, 'a little cold-blooded destruction warms the heart.' He stretched his legs. 'And in this case, the feet as well.'

Somehow it seemed like a symbolic gesture, as if they were burning what was bad between them. But it wasn't so easy. You could burn a book, but you couldn't burn truth. Or fear, or suspicion. But deep down inside her there was always that little spark of hope that was never quite extinguished. Sometimes it flared up and for a few precious moments everything seemed bright and happy between them and then something happened and the light died down and she was again engulfed in the grey dimness of despondency.

It was the uncertainty that got to her, the never knowing from day to day whether it made any sense at all to be here. Was she only torturing herself? Seeing him every day, loving him, longing for his love, yet knowing she couldn't reach him, knowing they grew farther apart as time went by—how long could she take it?

The frustration ate at her. Feeling helpless, powerless and out of control was not something she knew how to deal with. In the past, whenever she had had a problem, she had always known how to arrive at a solution. There was always something she could do, but not so now. All she could do now was wait and she didn't know how long she could bear it.

The next day a two-hour drive through green countryside bathed in warm sunshine brought them to Nairobi.

'Meet me at the New Stanley for lunch,' Vic said,

looking at his watch. 'Let's say about noon.' He pointed the hotel out to her, then left her to go to his meeting.

The next few hours Amy wandered around on her own, marvelling at the sight of the tall modern buildings, the wide avenues, the beautiful stores. So this was part of Africa, too—this clean, Western city full of sophisticated people—African men in suits and ties, women wearing the latest fashions. It seemed light years away from the mud-hut village and the people who lived there.

But as she walked farther away from the centre of town, the buildings grew older and smaller and the surroundings took on a more foreign atmosphere. There were all manner of small shops, many of which seemed to be run by Asians, and the strong fragrances of incense and exotic Indian spices filled her nostrils.

She loved it. She loved this place. She peered into the shop windows with eager fascination, looking over the displays of gold and silver jewellery, vibrantly coloured fabrics, brass and copper ornaments. Where did all that stuff come from? A pirate ship? A fairy tale treasure chest?

Outside the shop entrances dark-eyed children played around big burlap bags full of lentils, beans, grains and spices, most of which she couldn't identify. Her fingers itched to make sketches, to catch on paper the feeling, the atmosphere of the place, but all she had with her was her camera and as unobtrusively as she could, she took some pictures.

Two women in saris floated past her, chattering in some Asian language. It was amazing, Amy thought, to think that most of these people had been born in Africa and had never even seen the country of their heritage. To think that after several generations they still dressed and talked and ate like their great-grandparents who'd come to Kenya to build the Kampala-Mombasa railway. To think that they were so strictly bound by caste, custom and tradition that mingling with the Africans was impossible. Well, it made for an interesting, colourful society, she thought, with tension flourishing like weeds, no doubt.

She bought some dried figs tied together on a string and chewing them one by one she began to wind her way back to the centre of town, stopping to look here and there, taking her time.

She arrived at the New Stanley earlier than she had expected and she sat on the terrace watching the world go by, a parade of people in all shades and colours— Africans, Europeans, Asians, wearing all manner of clothes. People in suits and shorts and saris, bearded Sikhs in turbans, dark-eyed Pakistani girls wearing loose trousers and tight tunics, gauzy shawls draped around their shoulders. Fragments of conversations in many languages floated through the air.

She didn't mind waiting; she wasn't bored, but not much later her eyes caught sight of Vic shouldering his way through the masses in search of lunch. Somehow you never really had to look for Vic. If he was there, you saw him. Tall and wide-shouldered, he stood out in any crowd. As she watched him stride across the street, she noticed how much he seemed to belong here. Confident and self-assured, he was a man of the world, at home anywhere.

He walked right up to her and she realised he had located her well before he'd reached the terrace. He greeted her and sat down, stretching out his legs in front of him. He took off his sunglasses and slid them into the breast pocket of his jacket.

'We don't have to eat here,' he said. 'I know a place where they make a good curry. How adventurous are you?'

'I'm *here*, aren't I?'

A slight pause. A strange look in his eyes. 'No doubt about that.'

'I didn't come to Africa to eat hamburgers, you

know,' she said, quoting him, and he laughed.

'You probably didn't expect curry either.'

'If it tastes anything like those *samosas* I had at Bunny's place, I'll need a few glasses of water to douse the fires in my stomach!'

The curry tasted like nothing she had ever eaten before. Hot and spicy, it had no resemblance to the watered-down versions she had eaten at home. It was like eating fire, with smoke coming out of her ears and nose, or so it felt.

Afterwards they walked to one of the art stores to show the manager Amy's sketches. She felt jittery with nervous anticipation, gathering courage only from the fact that Vic was with her. She felt like a four-year-old coming to school for the first time, clinging to its mother's skirts, hiding behind her. She wanted to hide behind Vic when they entered the shop, but he gently pushed her ahead of him through the door.

The manager was an Indian, wearing a black suit and tie and a white shirt, and the mournful expression on his face made him look as if he were on his way to a funeral.

My funeral, Amy thought. The funeral of my self-esteem, my confidence (whatever there was of it). From the wall a huge wooden mask gaped at her with hollow eyes, doing nothing to cheer her up.

But her fears were unjustified. The man was all smiles, all compliments when he saw her work. He would be *most* delighted to have her work on sale, he said. There were other things he said, but Amy didn't hear them.

Back outside in the sunshine, she couldn't contain her elation. She felt like singing or dancing, and in a sudden impulsive gesture she threw her arms around Vic's neck and hugged him.

'Oh, Vic! He liked my pictures!'

'Of course.' His eyes were laughing down into hers. 'I told you so.'

For a moment Amy was oblivious to everything around her, aware only of his face so close to hers, feeling again her love for him welling up inside her.

'Thank you,' she said softly. 'Thank you, Vic.'

His eyebrows shot up. 'For what?'

'For boosting my courage, my self-confidence.'

He shook his head and smiled. 'You're funny,' he said, and there was warmth in his voice. 'Come on, let's go.'

It was there again—that sense of closeness they once knew. Shared joy and understanding. Exhilaration made her step light and it seemed as if she were floating through the air. Their reflection shimmered in the wide glass panes of the shop windows and she liked what she saw—a tall, wide-shouldered man in a khaki suit; a slim girl with dark shiny hair swinging loose around her shoulders, her face glowing.

We look good together, she thought. This was life and love and happiness—walking down these streets bustling with exotic-looking people, being here with the man she loved, who believed in her and shared her joy.

They stopped in front of a bookstore and Vic opened the door. 'I have to pick up a book for Tanya;' he said, stepping aside to let her in. 'You haven't met her yet, have you?'

Tanya. With a sickening thud Amy landed back to earth and the crystal glow of her happiness shattered to a thousand tiny fragments. A dull despair filled her. How could she forget? For a few moments she had lived a fantasy and now she was back to the reality of life.

'Tanya? No ... I mean yes, I did meet her.'

He seemed surprised. 'She wasn't at the party.'

It seemed difficult to speak. 'She came to the house the day after I arrived to drop off a towel you'd left at her place.' The words came automatically as if someone else were speaking them. She looked at him, trying not to show her emotions, and she saw him frowning.

'So that's where it came from. I wondered what it was doing there in the living room.' His face was smooth again, his voice level. He walked up to the counter and asked if the ordered book had arrived from the States yet. It had. It was a biology textbook, she saw.

'Why is she buying her own book?' she asked when they were outside again.

He shrugged. 'I'm not sure. There's something in it she wants to use. She likes to do things her own way as much as she can get away with.' He smiled. 'She's something special.'

The day had lost its shine. Amy's gaiety was gone. The bright and colourful world around her suddenly seemed flat and dull, and a sense of doom settled on her spirit.

There was one more item to add to the list of Tanya's qualities—'*She's something special.*' And this one had come straight from Vic himself.

You're crazy, she told herself the next day. Here you are, sitting on your knees, weeding out Vic's *shamba*, breaking your nails and ruining your back. Good for you, a little voice answered. Weed your brain, while you weed the broccoli. Get your thoughts and feelings in order, in nice, neat, straight lines, like the garden.

It felt good to dig around in the moist earth, feeling the warmth of the sun on her bare limbs and back. Shorts and a halter top was all she had on; she might as well get a tan while she was labouring away here. Her skin was naturally dark and she tanned easily, without burning.

Sunshine had followed the rains and weeds were everywhere ready to choke the vegetables. Kariuki had started the cleaning process, but hadn't finished. For an hour or so she worked and then, satisfied with what she had accomplished, she went inside.

She took a cold bath and washed her hair. She felt invigorated. Physical labour was good once in a while, but it did play havoc with one's appearance. She grimaced at the sight of her hands—broken nails and rough skin. She filed all her nails short and removed the remnants of the polish. Who needed to be glamorous in a mud-hut village?

In the afternoon she went for a walk. She felt restless, like a caged cat. Lack of activity was starting to bother her. In school at home little kids had very effective ways of keeping her running most of the time. They beat each other up, they spilled paint, they wet their pants by accident. She missed them, like she missed them every summer vacation. Her sister Laura said she was crazy. Have mine for the summer, she said. *Keep* them. Laura had three children—monsters, spoiled rotten. She loved them dearly, but only when they were in school or asleep in bed.

The village seemed quiet; no children following her this time. She was walking fast, getting rid of excess energy. She was on the path that led to the main road when she saw a young boy coming towards her on a bicycle. He smiled and stopped beside her.

'Good afternoon,' he said. *Awfternoon.* Beautiful English—proper, perfect.

'Hi,' she said—not so beautiful, not so perfect.

'How are you?' he asked in the same well-enunciated tone.

'I am fine, thank you.' It sounded as if they were reading from an English textbook for beginners.

'My name is Kamau.'

Nice boy, intelligent face. 'I'm Amy. Do you live in the village?'

He nodded. 'But I'm going away to boarding school soon. And when I'm finished there, I want to go to a university and become an engineer.'

An engineer. An ambitious kid, this one. Couldn't be more than twelve or thirteen.

'What kind of engineer?' she asked.

'A civil engineer, like Mr Hoyt. He says I am very clever and that I can do it if I study very hard.'

Vic was making friends, and not only with adults. 'I'm sure he's right,' Amy smiled.

'Mr Hoyt is a very fine man,' he said pompously. 'He repaired our water pump and he let me help. It was broken for two years, but he knew how to fix it.'

'You speak English very well,' said Amy, wondering how to finish off the discussion and get on with her walk.

'I study very hard,' he said gravely. Then he smiled. 'Would you like to see my *shamba*?'

'Sure.' Why not?

A field of corn, rows of peas, a patch of potatoes. His mother and sister worked in the *shamba*, he said. His father owned a little *duka*. Amy wasn't quite sure how it all happened, but before she realised it, she'd agreed to meet his mother and the next thing she knew she was led into a small wooden house where Kamau's smiling mother served her a plate of food. Sitting on the only available chair, Amy stared at the enormous mound of greenish something, panic rising to her throat.

I can't possibly eat this, she thought in terror. It's more than I eat in three days. *'You may never refuse food.'* Somewhere along the line Vic had told her that, she didn't remember when. But the knowledge was there, stored in her brain.

'What is it?' she asked Kamau, regretting the question instantly. She might be better off not knowing.

The woman smiled. Kamau smiled.

'Irio,' he said, as if that explained everything. She stared at the food helplessly, incapable of picking up her spoon and digging into it. 'I've never had this before,' she said weakly.

'It is very good,' Kamau assured her.

Of course it was good. Nobody in his right mind

would give a special guest something that wasn't. This greenish stuff was delicious, couldn't she *see* that? No preservatives, no artificial colourings or flavourings— the real thing. The only problem was that they were dealing with a difference in perceptions, a difference in culture and background. She came from a place where people ground and pressed together all manner of unmentionables, called them *hot dogs*, and ate them, pretending it was food. Now that was good.

I'd sell my soul for a hot dog, Amy thought miserably. Or even boiled spinach. Hopefully, she looked up at the ceiling, but no help was coming from above. Gathering all her courage, she scooped some food on to her spoon. There was only one way to get through this nightmare—eat. She ate.

It was not as bad as she had expected. It was bland and rather tasteless, as if someone had forgotten to put in the salt. But it was terribly dry and hard to swallow. Potatoes, she realised, mostly potatoes, mashed with peas and greens of some sort. She didn't detect anything exotic and she was relieved. Now if only it wasn't so terribly dry. Then she was handed a glass of milk— hot milk, but she didn't care. Anything to help swallow the starchy mass down. There seemed to be no end to it. She swallowed spoon after spoon and there was always more.

Almost gagging, her stomach extended until she thought it would burst, she finally finished. Oh God, she moaned inwardly, I'm going to die. This is the worst thing that's ever happened to me in my life.

She made it home, but how she didn't know, aware only of the agonising pain in her stomach. Bent over, her hand on her abdomen, she staggered into her bedroom and dropped on the bed like a sack of sand. A burning sensation flamed through her skin and crying out in pain she sat up again. Sunburn? It couldn't be, she thought in amazement. She didn't burn that easily. She'd only been out for an hour this morning! But one look at her arms convinced her—sunburn all right. Too busy with her digestive distress, she had not noticed the burning glow of her skin.

It was all she needed. With tears rolling down her cheeks, she slowly lowered herself on to her side. It was too much. She cried with frustration, furious at herself, at her own stupidity. And when there was a knock on her door she knew it had to be Vic. Murphy's law—everything that *can* go wrong, *will* go wrong.

'Go away!' she called out in a choked voice. But of course he could hear that she was crying and she wasn't surprised that he stood next to her bed a minute later.

'Go away,' she repeated.

'I've just got here. Good God, what have you done to yourself?' he demanded.

'Nothing! I did nothing *to* myself! It all just happened to me.'

'Sunburn doesn't just *happen*.'

'Well, it did! I was only out for about an hour! I never burn like this—I don't know why it happened! And why don't you just leave me in peace!'

'It might have something to do with the altitude and the latitude of this place. I'll get something and put it on you.'

Amy moaned. 'Never mind my skin. My stomach—I need something for that first.'

'Your stomach? Are you sick?'

'Dying. I have a ton of *irio* in me.'

'*Irio?*' His eyebrows shot up. Vic threw back his head and the warm, deep sound of his laughter filled the little room. 'Kikuyu hospitality got you, right?'

His amusement incensed her. First John, now this! With a jerk she sat upright, forgetting about the pain, wincing as she felt her aching body's protest.

'I can do without your laughing at me!' she said furiously. 'Why don't you get lost? I don't need you!'

'Like hell you don't.' He was smiling now. 'You're a basket case, and we'd better do something.' He left the room, coming back a few minutes later with a glass of bubbly liquid and an aerosol can.

'Sit up and drink this,' he ordered.

She did.

'Now turn around and take off your shirt.'

She had no choice, so she did as he requested, saying nothing.

'Your bra, too.'

'No!'

Without further ado, he did it for her, his cool hands lightly touching her burning skin.

'You didn't have to do that! It wasn't necessary!' She was looking at the wall, not wanting to turn around and face him. Tears of misery, pain, and humiliation filled her eyes.

'Don't be an idiot. Lobsters don't turn me on.' He sprayed her back with the can and the coolness soothed the pain instantly. Then he reached over her shoulder and dropped the can unceremoniously into her lap. 'Here, you can do the rest yourself.' He was out of the room before she could say anything.

She didn't eat dinner, only joined Vic for a cup of coffee in front of the fire. He asked her for the details of her culinary adventure, which she gave him, promising herself that she'd kick his shins if he laughed at her again. He didn't. He only smiled, which wasn't quite enough justification to attack him.

'They were only trying to make you feel welcome,' he explained.

'I never knew that being welcome could be such a painful experience.' She drank her coffee, thought of Kamau, his mother working in the field. 'Kamau wants to become an engineer, like you.'

'He's a super-smart kid. If he wants to, he'll make it.'

Look at us, she thought derisively. We look like a pair of octogenarians. All we need is a couple of rocking chairs and a cat asleep at our feet. Oh, God, I can't stand this. I can't stand the way we are together.

She wanted Vic to put his arms around her, hold her. She wanted him to love her. But tomorrow was Thursday. Tomorrow he would see Tanya.

He stood up abruptly, saying he had work to do. He turned his back, leaving her alone with her thoughts.

Why don't I go home? she thought miserably. Or better yet, why don't I shoot myself?

She went to bed early, and sobbing silently into the pillow, cried herself to sleep.

'I'll be gone for the night,' Vic said at breakfast. 'If you want, I'll drive you into town. I'm sure Bunny would love to have you.'

Something snapped inside her. All emotion drained from her, leaving her empty and cold. So he wasn't just going to see Tanya; he was going to stay at her house for the night. Somehow she managed to keep her composure, telling him in calm tones that she was fine right here, that she wasn't afraid to be alone any more. She wanted to work on some sketches, she said. Besides, Nyeri was probably out of the way and it wasn't necessary, really.

This was the moment she had feared. She could take no more. And now nothing seemed to matter any more. Vic could go see his terrific Tanya, and as for her, there was only one thing to do.

Go home.

CHAPTER SIX

SHE watched him drive away down the dirt track, a cloud of red dust engulfing his Land Rover, taking it from her sight. 'Goodbye, Vic,' she said out loud. 'It was nice knowing you.' She went inside, dry-eyed. In her room she began packing away her things, folded her clothes, rolled up her drawings—all with automatic precision.

Kariuki didn't seem happy with her wish to leave, but she ignored his pleas and reluctantly he helped carry her bags to the road. She waited, shivering in the cool morning air. Surely somebody would come by and give her a ride into town? Hitch-hiking, she thought. My God, what's happening to me? She didn't have to wait long. A cloud of dust announced the arrival of a vehicle. It was a green sports car driven by a bearded Sikh wearing a white turban and Western sports clothes. He was young, handsome, and flashed her a smile that could light up a room.

He was more than pleased to take her to Nyeri, he said. He was sorry that he wasn't going to Nairobi today, but on Monday he was and it would be a pleasure, an *honour*, to have her company if she could wait until then. He smiled and laughed and paid her compliments, and Amy thought that Don Juan could have taken lessons from him. He drove as if he were on an American interstate freeway rather than an African dirt road and her heart pounded uneasily. But he seemed perfectly at ease, handling his car with skill and precision, and after a while Amy relaxed.

What was she going to do? She hadn't thought about anything but leaving the village. Maybe she should stay at Bunny's for the night, find out how to find a reasonable hotel in Nairobi, where to go to sign up for a safari through the game parks. She was here in Africa now, she might as well make the best of it, then, when she came home, she could at least impress her friends with her adventures.

As they drove into town, Amy realised that Bunny wouldn't be home until the afternoon. Damn, she thought, why don't I think before I jump? There was a restaurant somewhere nearby Bunny's apartment and she asked the man to drop her off there. She could sit on the terrace and have coffee, then have lunch later and maybe they wouldn't mind keeping her luggage while she walked around town to kill time.

'May I buy you a drink?' the man asked her as he helped her out of the car.

'Why don't *I* offer *you* something to drink, as thanks for your kindness?' she asked.

His smile collapsed. 'Certainly not! It was my pleasure to give you a lift and you offend me!'

Was he joking? 'Haven't you heard?' she asked.

He looked puzzled. 'Heard what?'

'Women's Lib is here.'

He raised his eyes heavenward. 'Oh, you European women!' He took her arm and led her to a table.

'I'm not European, I'm American.'

He shrugged. 'It's all the same here. All white people are called Europeans.'

His company helped pass the time, although Amy found his Don Juan routine irritating at best. He was sweet as maple syrup and treated her as if she were an exquisite, fragile china doll, all looks and no brains.

Was she quite sure she couldn't wait and come with him on Monday? She was positive, she said. She had to go tomorrow. He wanted to show her around, he said, teeth flashing in a hundred-watt smile. There were so many things to do in Nairobi.

She could imagine.

When he finally stood up to leave, he took out a business card, indicating his home phone number printed under the one for the office. 'Give me a ring some time, or if you need a place to stay....' He began to scribble his home address on the back of the card, then looked up, smiling invitingly. 'I have a very nice apartment.'

And a very nice bedroom, no doubt. Maybe even a water bed.

With a big wave he drove off, engine racing, wheels screeching.

'Thanks, but no thanks,' Amy said out loud, tearing up the card, dropping the pieces into the ashtray.

Bunny was delighted to see her. 'Stay as long as you want. I'm going to Nairobi myself next week—a party. We can go together. There's a whole empty bedroom upstairs, it's all yours.' She started up the stairs, then turned around halfway. 'Would you mind making some tea? I'll go change and rake my hair.'

She came back a while later wearing jeans and an orange T-shirt with a slogan printed on the front. NURSES DO IT ALL THE TIME, Amy read. It seemed a rather provocative proclamation to be carrying around on your chest. But then she'd seen worse.

'Like it?' Bunny asked, seeing Amy's expression. 'My father gave it to me.'

'Your *father*?'

Bunny grinned. 'He's one of a kind.'

'You don't say,' Amy said drily.

Over tea she told Bunny of her plans, but in the end she was persuaded to stay on through the next week. 'I'd love to have you,' Bunny assured her. 'Really. I like people around, I hate being alone.'

Amy knew that it would be futile to try not to think about Vic, but every time thoughts of him entered her consciousness she could feel her heart grow stone cold, her body rigid. She didn't want to waste her emotions on him any more. With iron self-control she kept away the tears, froze out the pain and anguish that kept surfacing. No more. No more. She had made a mistake and now she had to learn to live with it, or better still, forget it.

But she wasn't armed enough. She could defend herself against her thoughts of him—for a while. But when he appeared in the doorway that Friday afternoon, she knew there was no defence against the overwhelming power of his presence.

The sight of him alone was enough to wake her emotions from frozen sleep. With her heart hammering she stared at him standing in the door of the apartment. She hadn't expected to see him again, but there he was—dusty, dirty, unshaven. And furious.

'I thought I'd find you here.' He strode inside, slamming the door behind him. 'I want to talk to you.'

'Hello to you too,' Bunny said drily. She was sitting on the sofa, curled up with a book, watching the two of them.

'Sorry, didn't see you.'

'So I noticed.' She stood up. 'I just remembered, I have to get some bread. We're out.'

'There's a whole loaf on the counter,' said Amy. 'You don't have to leave.'

Bunny frowned. 'We have bread? Maybe it was sugar, then. Or margarine. We must be out of something, I'm sure.' She swung out of the door, leaving them facing each other.

'I don't know why you're here,' Amy said, and meant it.

'You don't?' Vic put his hand in his pocket, took out the note and the bills she had left and threw them on the table. 'What the hell is this supposed to mean?'

'The money?'

'Yes, the money! Among other things.'

She shrugged. 'Just as I said: to pay for my keep.'

'Don't be absurd!'

'Absurd? I don't think so. There's no need for you to pay for my food. I didn't come here to sponge off you. I don't like being in anyone's debt—I prefer to pay my own way.'

The corners of his mouth turned down. 'You didn't seem to mind my paying for our entertainment back home.'

'That was different.'

'Oh? How was that different?'

'I was invited!'

There was a momentary silence and a strange expression swept across his face.

'I see.'

She didn't know what else to say. She began to stack teacups and saucers. Maybe he would go away. She wanted him to leave, and still at the same time she wished he would stay. He was staring at her, she could tell. He sighed, but she refused to look up at him.

'There's something going on that I don't understand,' he said. 'Why did you leave in such a hurry? Couldn't you have waited until I got back?'

She shrugged again. 'I just felt it was time to go. I didn't think it mattered particularly.'

'You're not making sense, you know.'

'Neither do you!' she snapped.

'Why do I have the feeling there's something more involved?' he asked, and she looked up, seeing him standing there, hands in his pockets, eyes dark.

'Don't ask me. I haven't a clue.'

'Don't you?'

'No!' She was impatient, angry, scared. 'I don't understand why you drove up here all the way from the village. I don't understand why you make such a fuss about a lousy hundred shillings!'

'Is that what I'm doing?'

She gritted her teeth. 'Seems to me like it.'

'It seems to me that *you're* the one who's hung up about money. You know damn well that a few meals aren't going to ruin me, not even on a Peace Corps allowance.'

'*I'm* hung up about money?' she said hotly. '*Me?*'

He nodded. 'Why are you so afraid to be in my debt, as you call it?'

Amy glared at him, clenching her hands. 'I'm not *afraid* to be in your debt,' she said furiously. 'I'm only paying my own way. You're not used to that, are you? You're always doing the buying and the paying and the giving. Well, *I* don't need it!'

He moved towards her and she backed away, but he quickly caught her by the shoulders. His eyes magnetised her and she couldn't look away. He held her gaze for a few silent moments.

'What are you trying to prove?' he asked slowly. His tone seemed deceptively calm, but there was an undertone of something else. Frustration? Anger?

'I'm not trying to prove anything!' She wrenched herself away from his grip, picked up the cups and walked to the kitchen. 'Why don't you go home?' she said over her shoulder. Vic followed her into the kitchen, ignoring the remark. 'Are you still afraid I might think you came here to chase me and my money?'

Amy whirled around, livid. 'I don't care what you think! The audacity! You ... you think you're so special because of your money—well, forget it! *I* don't happen to think a lot of money is necessarily such a blessing! *I* don't need it. There's nothing money can buy me that I'm dying to have!'

'Oh? Is that so?' He stood there, calmly leaning against the counter, observing her with a mingling of interest and faint amusement. His expression enraged her even further.

'Yes, that is so! I have a job I like, my self-respect, and I can stand on my own two feet. You tell me what else I should need!'

'How about love?'

She stared at him in stunned silence.

'Well?' he demanded.

'Love isn't something you buy with money, although *you* may think differently.'

His face hardened, suddenly, and his eyes narrowed dangerously. 'You're not making sense,' he said slowly. 'If I'm so in love with money, why am I not out there making it?'

'How should I know? I'm not your analyst, so don't ask me to explain that warped mind of yours! I seem to remember you once said something about being bored. Maybe you need a little diversion from the stresses of American business life, something you can tell funny stories about and amuse your friends with when you get back home....'

She'd hit him on the raw. His face turned to stone and his grey eyes were filled with an icy cold rage. Blinded by tears, she whirled around and ran up the stairs to her room, threw herself on the bed and lay there, curled up in misery. She hadn't meant it; she hadn't meant what she'd said. She was only lashing out at him to hurt, and she knew it. But it didn't feel good. It didn't feel good at all. Her stomach churned— anger, pain, fear, it was all there. It was as if she were sinking away into a bottomless pit of misery, deeper and deeper until it washed over her in waves and she was drowning in it.

'I *dare* you to repeat that!'

She stiffened. Vic had followed her and he was looking down on her as she lay on the bed facing the wall, tears streaming down into the pillow.

She lay very still and didn't answer.

He hauled her over into a sitting position. 'Answer me!'

Amy covered her face with her hands. 'I'm sorry. I'm sorry,' she whispered. 'I didn't mean it.' Tears were trickling through her fingers and she felt a helpless desperation fill her heart.

'Good!'

Then he was gone. She heard his footsteps going down the stairs. The front door slammed, hard. She was alone.

Bleakly she got off the bed, washed her face, combed her hair. She looked a mess; she *was* a mess. As she went down the stairs, she heard Bunny come in the door. She gave Amy a searching look, but made no comment.

'Would you like some coffee? I bought some cookies.'

Amy smiled weakly. 'You didn't have to leave, you know.'

Bunny grinned. 'Actually, I almost turned back. Vic looked so mad I wondered if my presence might not be needed to prevent a murder.' She walked to the kitchen and Amy followed her.

Bunny frowned as she put water in the kettle. 'I guess we should have dinner first—it's almost seven. Are you hungry?'

Amy shook her head. 'No.'

'Okay, to hell with dinner.' Bunny slapped herself on her hip. 'I could stand to lose a few pounds, anyway.'

After which statement she sat down, had coffee and demolished half a bag of cookies.

It wasn't hard to live with Bunny—not if you didn't mind a lot of clutter and noise and laughter. Not if you weren't too musical and could stand Bunny's voice. She sang in the kitchen, in the bathroom, everywhere—loud and off key. She sailed around in floating, flamboyant kaftans of the wildest colours and designs. She was full of off-colour jokes and dubious but hilarious hospital stories. She was a nursing teacher, but wanted to go back to nursing when she came home. Amy was convinced that Bunny with her joy and laughter could bring the dead back to life.

'Amy,' she said one afternoon, 'how would you like a

job? Stay here for a while?'

Amy gaped. 'A job?'

'I have a friend, she runs a nursery school and she needs help desperately. I told her about you and she wants to come and talk to you tonight. You could stay here with me, at least until the Peace Corps wants to put someone else in with me, and the school isn't too far away, you could walk, and it could be fun....' Bunny sounded like a train.

'Wait a minute!' It was going too fast for her. 'Tell me, who is that friend?'

'Katherine—Katherine Wangai. She's Kenyan, a fabulous teacher, I think so anyway. It's a private school and she started it herself. It's small and she wants to keep it that way. Wait till you see her, she's gorgeous.'

Katherine was gorgeous all right. Amy stared at her as she entered the apartment later that evening. She was tall, slender, very dark and strikingly beautiful. She looked more like a New York City fashion model than a teacher, and totally unlike what Amy would have expected a friend of Bunny's to look like.

She came to the point without much ado. There was a shortage of qualified teachers, she said, so she had hired two girls who had all the makings of good teachers, but didn't have the paper qualifications. They needed some professional guidance and training and would Amy want to think about that? It would be a temporary position—how long, she couldn't say at this point.

Was there anything to think about? She *had* to do this. It was a challenge, an opportunity she might never get again. Yes, she said, she'd *love* to do it.

The next morning she wrote a letter of resignation to her school at home. No guilty feelings, thank God. The substitute teacher would have her job—she'd wanted to start again full time.

She walked to the post office, mailed the letter,

walked out of the building into the sun-filled street
and it was as if lightning hit her. I did it again, she
thought in horror. In my infinite stupidity I acted on
impulse again.

Last night it had all sounded so wonderful—a nice
little school, lots of toys and teaching materials, all
kinds of children—European, African, Asian. But why
hadn't she taken some time to think about it? Find out
what else was involved?

Because she hadn't wanted to think about it, that
was why. Her instincts had told her that this was what
she wanted and she hadn't allowed her rational mind
to enter into the decision.

Back at the apartment she made herself some coffee,
sat down on the sofa, stared at a stack of magazines a
foot high. She took a sip from her coffee—yuk, it was
weak and watery. She got up, walked to the kitchen,
poured the coffee down the sink and stared out the
window. I'm still hanging on, she thought miserably. I
took that job because I don't want to leave. Oh, God,
what am I going to do?

It soon became apparent that there was one thing
she wasn't going to do—stay out of Vic's way. He came
to the apartment again late Friday afternoon, clean
and shaven, wearing lightweight grey slacks and a
dark blue shirt. He greeted her coolly, handing her a
letter.

'This was in the mail for you.

'Thanks.'

He dumped his overnight bag on the floor and sat
down in a chair.

'What are you doing here?' Amy asked.

He threw her a mocking glance. 'I'm staying here for
the night.'

Oh, he was, was he? His eyes were taunting her, but
she said nothing, stared back at him in silence.

'I met Bunny at the post office,' he said. 'She told
me the two of you are going to Nairobi tomorrow and

I said I was on my way there today. Then she tempted me with a free meal, her inspiring company and the use of her lumpy couch. So I'll stay and we'll all go tomorrow.'

'I haven't decided yet whether I'll go or not.'

He ignored her remark, gave her a level gaze. 'I told Bunny you were out of bread.'

'You're so smart,' she said coolly. 'What do you want to talk about now?' But she knew, oh yes, she knew.

'Bunny told me you've accepted a teaching job,' Vic remarked.

'Yes, I have. Any objections? Did I do something wrong again?'

'Something wrong? Don't be so damn naïve!' Impatiently he jumped up from his chair, stood in front of her, hands on his hips. 'Don't you understand? You can't just get yourself a job here! It's illegal!'

Anger surged through her and she clenched her hands into fists. 'Listen,' she said with barely constrained fury, 'I wish you'd mind your own business! I'm quite capable of taking care of myself. From the moment I set foot in this country you've been putting me down, and I've had enough of it!' She whirled around, but he caught her wrist and turned her back to face him. His eyes glinted hard as steel.

'You stay right here until I'm finished with you,' he gritted.

'You're hurting me!'

'Good. Maybe you'll listen to me then.'

She couldn't believe it. She couldn't believe that this was the same man she'd known at home, that warm, courteous, gentle man she had fallen in love with. He had changed beyond recognition and still she loved him. Still there was that deep, aching hunger inside her every time she saw him—a longing for his love, his touch, a longing that went beyond doubt, beyond reason.

He did not let go of her wrist and his grip hurt her, it really did hurt. His face was blurred and so was the rest of the room.

'Please let me go,' she said meekly. 'I'll listen.'

'All right.' He hooked his thumbs behind his belt and straightened his back. 'The woman that offered you the job, Mrs Wangai, did she say anything about a work permit?'

'No.'

'I was afraid of that.' He sighed. 'They have an unemployment rate of forty-five per cent or so in this country. One thing that doesn't help is foreigners taking jobs.'

'I'm not really taking a job away from anybody! I'm going to help out by training a couple of girls to be better teachers! It's only temporary and I get hardly any money at all!'

'The law may not see the distinction. You've got to make sure that Mrs Wangai clears your situation legally or you could find yourself in deep trouble.'

Deep trouble? How deep? Would they throw her in front of the lions? Put her in jail? Deport her? Possibilities to be avoided, definitely.

'Okay, I'll ask her,' she said lamely, disliking herself for crumbling under his words, his steely grey eyes. He had done it again. She felt small and dumb. But he was right and she couldn't feel angry about it, just dispirited and helpless. He's looking after me, she thought bleakly, and I don't want him to. I don't want to need him so.

She wished she could walk away from him, be free of him. Not think about him any more. Not love him any more. But he had become too much a part of her, of her life, her dreams, her hopes. How could she cut him out now?

'I'm going to make some coffee. You want some?' Her voice was flat and lifeless and she didn't look at him.

'Please.'

He followed her into the kitchen and somehow she'd known he would. She filled the kettle and turned on the stove, moving automatically with everything still blurred in front of her. There was a strange silence and there were no words to fill it, and when his arms came around her she didn't resist. He turned her slowly, gently, and he made not a sound and said not a word. With her eyes closed she leaned against him, and the strength and the warmth and the scent of him filled her, and the world faded away.

He kissed her, and it was different than it ever had been. It had the quality of a dream, unreal and fleeting. It happened in a separate space of time, a different level of consciousness, not touching reality.

And when the shrill whistle of the kettle broke the spell, it seemed that in some strange and incomprehensible way everything, and nothing, had changed.

Vic reached for the cups. 'I'll help you.'

Amy lifted the kettle and turned off the stove. She felt slightly dazed as if she had just woken up from a deep sleep. Sleeping Beauty kissed awake by the prince, she thought derisively.

'Instant?' the prince asked, and she almost smiled. Princes didn't drink coffee in fairy tales. They drank wine from silver goblets. Vic was no prince, no prince at all. And she was no beauty for that matter, asleep or awake.

'I don't like instant,' she said, tossing her hair behind her shoulders. 'I'll drip some.'

'Make it strong, I need it.'

So he had felt it too. Had she doubted it?

They heard the front door open.

'Howdy! I'm home!' Bunny entered the kitchen carrying a large pineapple. Her face was solemn, but her eyes were laughing. 'Sorry I'm late,' she said, 'but I remembered just in time that we were out of bread.' With a great flourish she deposited the pineapple on the counter top and grinned.

*

Vic hadn't said why he was going to Nairobi and Amy hadn't asked. There was no reason for her to go now that she was not leaving for home, but Bunny insisted she come, and in the end she was glad she did. Diversion was what she needed and diversion was what she got. Bunny knew a lot of people, or maybe it was that a lot of people knew Bunny, Amy wasn't sure which. Somehow that Saturday night they ended up at a large party in one of the ritzy residential neighbourhoods of the city. Amy never found out who the host was. There were all kinds of people—Kenyans, Asians, Europeans, all mingling together in joyful brotherhood warmed by the liberally flowing liquor. Amy talked to a strange assortment of individuals—a glassy-eyed Italian guitarist who roamed the world and sang on street corners to earn his daily bread or rice or beans; a Sikh who had studied in Texas and spoke with a Southern drawl; a big-bosomed Danish girl who smoked a pipe.

The Italian guitarist was trying to cosy up to her, but Amy wasn't charmed. By the looks of him he was higher than a kite on something—pot, whatever. He was enthralled by her name and kept repeating it like a child trying out a new word.

'Amy Morelli. Morelli! Morelli! Your name, it is Italian!' His look of exultation was something to behold, as if he'd made the discovery of the century.

'How about that,' she said coolly, sipping from a glass of wine she'd been nursing for an hour.

He slid to the floor, leaned against the side of a chair and began to talk to her in rapid Italian, his face radiating bliss.

She cut him short. 'I'm sorry, but I don't understand what you're saying. It's all Greek to me.'

He gaped. 'It's Italian!' He swallowed hard. 'I have not spoken Italian for two months.' He looked as if he was about to cry. 'Morelli, Morelli—are you sure you do not speak Italian?'

'I'm sorry to disappoint you. My grandparents were Italian immigrants. *I* am American, as in Campbell soup, the Statue of Liberty, King Kong. . . .' Seeing his face, she waved her hand. 'Never mind. But no, I don't speak Italian, at least not enough for an intelligent conversation.'

He looked sad. 'You are interested in intelligent conversations?'

'Only when I'm bored.'

Silence. He was trying to work out that one. It might take a while. Amy took the opportunity to smile at him sweetly and deliver her closing line.

'I only know three words,' she said. 'Spaghetti, pizza, and *ciao*!' She walked off. The world was full of jerks —dumb, hot-to-trot, or spaced-out like this character, and it wasn't any better here than at home.

She went in search of Bunny and found her in the company of a Japanese businessman, talking about Zen Buddhism, of all things.

Here's your intelligent discussion, Amy thought drily, listening to them talk about the mind being liberated and illuminated by transcendental wisdom, meditation, self-contemplation; about attaining mental tranquillity. Just what I need, she decided, thinking about Vic and her own very un-tranquil mental state. After a few minutes she moved away, just in time to hear the man declare that he himself was a Catholic, because it was more convenient and so universal. His statement nearly floored her. *Convenient!* As if faith were an American Express credit card—universally accepted, welcomed anywhere. Jerk, she thought, then smiled. A party was to be enjoyed. What she needed was another glass of wine. Some good company might help. She wished Vic was there. No, she didn't. Could she never stop thinking about him?

An Englishman rescued her from her miserable contemplations, offered to get her another glass of wine, and talked to her for the rest of the evening. He was neither drunk, spaced-out, or dumb. He was nice, really nice, his English clean and clipped, his conversation intelligent.

Amy had an enjoyable weekend and there was no room for boredom in the company of Bunny and her cronies. She didn't see Vic. He was somewhere in town, but she had no idea where, and she hadn't asked. All she knew was that he was staying on until Monday and she and Bunny had to find their own way back to Nyeri. Which they did, riding very comfortably in the flashy car of one of Bunny's friends who was on his way to Nanyuki.

Monday. Bunny went back to work. Amy stayed in bed until ten, feeling guilty and lazy, which didn't keep her from enjoying it. Later she went to see Katherine Wangai and asked her about a work permit, saying that her enthusiasm for the job did not stand up against the risk of deportation.

Katherine laughed. There was nothing to worry about, she said. Her husband was taking care of it. It would be all straightened out before school started.

There was no reason not to believe her. Katherine offered coffee and they talked some more—about the school, the teachers, the children. Amy's worries vanished, her enthusiasm grew. She liked Katherine, her approach, her attitude. She would get along with her just fine, she thought as she walked back to the apartment.

She hadn't expected to see Vic again until at least Friday when he'd come to town to get his mail, but he arrived that evening just as they sat down to eat their dinner.

'Sit down, have something to eat,' Bunny ordered, and he did, digging in with enthusiasm.

'You didn't cook this,' he said to Bunny, and it was a statement, not a question. 'It's delicious.'

Bunny looked wounded. 'I don't need any cracks about my cooking! But you're right, I didn't fix this.

Amy did. She's decided she'll do all the cooking, which is fine by me.'

'Amy is a smart girl,' he said. 'She'd like to survive this ordeal of sharing an apartment with you.' He was grinning maliciously and Bunny, for once, had no immediate retort.

'You just wait,' she said helplessly, 'God will get you for this.'

He laughed and turned to Amy. 'I have something for you,' he said, and took a folded envelope from his breast pocket and handed it to her.

Bunny began to clear the table. 'I'll make some coffee,' she said, giving Vic a threatening look. 'And my coffee is not bad.'

'You're right,' he said, smiling benevolently.

The envelope contained a cheque from the art gallery for all four of Amy's charcoal sketches. Speechlessly she stared at the amount, then she looked up, gathering her wits.

'All that money?'

'A German tourist bought all four,' he said.

'How did you know?'

'I didn't. I stopped by there this morning and they told me. They gave me the cheque to deliver it to you.'

'Do they want more?' she asked.

'Is the Pope Catholic?'

Amy shrugged. 'Well, I guess I don't have to worry how I'll support myself. The teaching salary isn't exactly up to American standards.'

'Which reminds me, did you talk to Katherine Wangai about a work permit?'

Immediately she felt on the defensive, her body stiffening in response. 'Her husband is taking care of it,' she said in a tight voice.

There was a short silence. Bunny came back with the coffee, handing each of them a cup. Vic looked at Amy, his face expressionless.

'Have you considered the fact that you'll be out of

work when you get back home? Teaching jobs aren't easy to get, you know that.'

She could feel her face tighten. He made her feel like a little girl having to justify herself to her daddy, and she didn't like it. She didn't want an argument, but he seemed determined to pressure her into one. She clenched her teeth and glared at him.

'Yes! I'll be out of work. I'll lose my apartment. I'll be hungry. I'll sleep on a park bench, catch pneumonia and die. Anything else you want to add?'

A faint smile. 'No, the scenario is quite complete.'

Bunny let out an exasperated sigh. 'Will you stop bugging her, for Pete's sake! She's single, has no ties. She can afford to live dangerously! In ten years she'll be sitting at home with three kids and a dog and the only freedom she'll have is when she goes to the supermarket alone while Daddy babysits.'

Vic laughed. 'Okay, you made your point. End of discussion.'

It wasn't like him to drop something so easily. He must have read the expression on her face and knew she was coming close to the point of explosion, and he probably didn't savour the idea of a blow-out in front of a third party.

The tension had passed and Amy smiled at Bunny. 'Three kids and a dog, you said. What else do you see in my future?'

Bunny frowned as if considering the question in earnest.'

'A cat, I think. And perhaps a couple of canaries.'

August passed with rainy days and sunny days, and flowers bloomed in profusion, greenery turned greener. Amy kept herself busy preparing for school, learning Swahili, making sketches. Every Friday Vic came to town to do his shopping and to pick up his mail at the post office, and afterwards he would stop by the apartment. Sometimes there was a letter for Amy, sometimes not. Bunny always invited him to stay for dinner and he always accepted. As reciprocation he brought them large amounts of produce from his *shamba*, enough to last them through the week.

He was friendly and polite to Amy, but teased Bunny mercilessly, which she seemed to enjoy. There were no more confrontations and Amy was never alone with him, but at night after he left she couldn't sleep, lay awake for hours with memories and longings destroying her peace of mind.

School started in September, and Amy had looked forward to it with great anticipation. She loved getting back to the familiar smells of chalk and paper. She felt at home in the cheerful rooms filled with brightly painted furniture and cabinets well stocked with toys and teaching materials. The sound of laughing children was music to her ears. This was her world, her domain.

The children made up a spectrum of race and nationality. Watching them come to school the first day was an experience Amy would never forget. African children, immaculately dressed; European and American children in sturdy playclothes; Asian girls with eye make-up and nail polish wearing frilly, lacy dresses; Sikh boys with long braids tied on top of their heads. On the outside they all looked so different, on the inside they were all the same—a little scared, a little shy at this first day at school.

Amy loved them all, and a few days later her trained mind had sorted them out and she had got to know them. She knew the shy ones, the lively ones, the quiet ones, the trouble-makers, the talkers.

And then there was Ricky. He was happy and lively one moment and the next he was sitting quietly in a corner sucking his thumb. Something was wrong, her instincts told her so. Linda Muriuki, Ricky's teacher and one of the girls to be trained, had noticed it too. She didn't know what was wrong. Neither did

Katherine. She'd give it a little time; wait and see.

Amy enjoyed living with Bunny, and the weekends were never boring with a parade of volunteers streaming through the apartment. They were mostly males—Germans, Norwegians, Dutchmen, Englishmen, Canadians, Americans. They came for a shower, a meal, a night's lodging. They slept on the sofa or spread their sleeping bags out on the floor. They all had the common need for a sympathetic ear, a sounding-board for their complaints and ideas, a short respite from their lonely existence in the bush.

'Are you running a hotel?' Vic asked Bunny one day.

'No,' she said, shaking her head. 'It's more like a non-profit organisation—*Bunny's Barracks*. Right, Amy?'

Amy nodded. 'A charity.'

Vic smiled. 'Or a losing proposition, if you take into consideration the type of guests you have.'

'I'm not in it for monetary gain,' Bunny said haughtily. 'I'm doing it from the goodness of my heart.'

'You have a very big heart,' Vic said gravely.

Bunny gave him a complacent smile. 'Yes, I know.'

For a moment he said nothing, only smiled, and Amy watched him, wondering what he'd say next.

'How's your search coming along for that man of your dreams? Classy, rich, handsome—wasn't that it?'

Bunny grinned. 'Nothing yet. I can wait.'

'Sure you're not too picky?'

She looked indignant. 'Listen, I'm a good buy at any price. See what he'll be getting for his money—a manager for his home and household, a mother for his children. . . .'

'A lousy cook,' Vic interjected.

Bunny glared at him. 'I'll ignore that,' she said coolly. 'Where was I? Oh, yes. A manager for his house, a mother for his children, an ardent mistress, a private nurse for the family.' She smiled smugly. 'I don't intend to undersell myself.'

'You talk as if you're a piece of merchandise,' smiled Amy.

'Right,' Vic added. 'A sewing machine. One of those that can do it all—buttons, zippers, fancy stitches....'

Bunny was not perturbed. 'Life is business,' she said coolly. 'That's my philosophy.'

'Just watch out you don't end up in the bargain basement,' said Vic. 'On special.'

Bunny picked up a magazine and threw it at him. He ducked just in time.

Bunny and Tanya were great friends—Amy should have guessed. They were a matchless pair, their conversations resembling ping-pong games—jokes, puns and wisecracks bouncing back and forth with a swiftness that dazzled Amy. Tanya was witty, smart, and undeniably nice. Amy couldn't help but like her, and wished she didn't. It would be so much easier if she didn't. Once Tanya came to town with Vic, who apparently had been at her place the previous night. Amy gathered the knowledge from bits and pieces from their conversation. Maybe it's all innocent, she thought miserably. Maybe he just needed a place to stay because he was working in the area. She laughed at her own naïveté. You're pathetic, she told herself. You don't believe it for a minute. *Look* at her.

Whenever Tanya visited them Amy was miserable. Whenever Vic was there, she was miserable. In fact, she was miserable even when they weren't there.

One afternoon Tanya entered the apartment, dragging her feet, looking as if she'd climbed a mountain and rolled back down. She sagged into a chair like a limp rag doll and sighed.

'Boy, am I tired!'

'You look as if you *walked* to town,' Bunny commented.

Tanya shook her head, as if walking to town was a

serious possibility that needed to be denied. 'I came with Vic.'

'Did he make you *push* his Land Rover? Anyway, where is he? Where's your stuff? I thought you were staying here tonight.'

'Change of plan. I'm staying with Vic.'

It didn't make sense. One look at Bunny convinced Amy that she didn't understand either. Bunny looked at Tanya, frowning.

'Staying with him—*where*?' she asked, then quickly raised her hand. 'Never mind, I don't even want to know.'

Tanya's eyes widened in surprise. 'Didn't you know? He's got a house in town. I helped him move this afternoon.'

CHAPTER SEVEN

'You're kidding!' Bunny exclaimed. 'Why didn't he tell us?'

'He didn't know. He put in the request months ago and suddenly it got approved.' Tanya shook her head. 'You should've seen the place, it was filthy. I helped clean it up—you know how men are.'

Amy almost laughed out loud. Had Tanya any idea how Vic used to live? Somehow she doubted it. Hadn't he told her?

'What kind of place is it?' Bunny asked.

Tanya grinned. 'It's a small house, but *very luxurious*,' she said with intended exaggeration. 'It has electricity and running water. Imagine that!'

No reaction came from Bunny and Tanya gave her a dirty look. 'Of course,' she said sarcastically, 'some of us don't know what it means to do without. Some of us poor suffering volunteers get put into modern apartments in town.'

They were at it again. It was the kind of banter they liked—throwing insults at each other, or tearing people or situations to shreds with benevolent viciousness, trying to outdo each other. Amy hadn't said a word and was only half hearing the conversation, still trying to digest the news. So Vic had a house in town. And Tanya was staying with him tonight. She'd said it matter-of-factly, as if nobody would think anything of it. Well, nobody would, most likely.

She felt sick, and she had a headache, suddenly. Why couldn't she be calm and cool and accept the situation for what it was? Why did she go to pieces every time something like this happened? Where was her shell? Her rock wall? But shells broke and rock walls crumbled, especially the ones she erected around her own heart.

'I'll make some tea,' said Bunny. 'Is Vic coming?'

Tanya nodded. 'He's taking Kariuki home. He'll be back.' She turned to Amy. 'He has some mail for you, I think.' She smiled. 'He told me you sold some more sketches.'

'Yes.' It took an effort to smile, but Amy managed.

'May I see your pictures some time?'

'Sure. I have one here that's almost finished.' Amy walked over to a table by the window and picked up the sketch. It depicted a Kikuyu woman carrying a huge bundle of firewood on her bent back. Tanya looked at the picture, admiration lighting up her face.

'It's beautiful, it really is.'

She meant it; there was no doubt in Amy's mind that she was sincere. For a brief moment she closed her eyes, as if she wanted to block out something, only she wasn't sure what. Why did Tanya have to be so nice? Why couldn't she have been the nasty type so she could at least have spent her energies disliking her?

'Something wrong?' Tanya was looking at her, a puzzled expression in her clear blue eyes.

'I have a headache. I think I'll go lie down for a while.' Her room seemed like a good place to be. She didn't want to see Vic, not today. Seeing him and Tanya together was more than she would be able to deal with at the moment.

'Take some aspirin,' said Tanya, 'and I'll bring you up some tea when it's ready.'

'Thanks,' Amy murmured, and climbed the stairs, hearing someone come in the front door as she reached the landing. Vic? No, Jerry, one of the volunteers who passed through at regular intervals.

She lay down on the bed and stared up at the ceiling. It wasn't a real headache she had, but more a dark, gloomy feeling, a weight pressing down on her spirit.

A while later she heard Vic's voice and the deep

warm sound of his laugh. She closed her eyes, fighting the urge to go down and see him, be near him. And when the knock on the door came she realised how tense she was, her body rigid, her hands clenched into fists.

'Come in.' She sat up, folding her legs tailor-fashion, then took a deep breath and relaxed her muscles. A cup of tea would do her good. A couple of shots of whisky would be better.

But it wasn't Tanya who came in, as she had expected. It was Vic, a cup in his hand, his eyes searching her face.

'You're not sick, are you?' he asked.

'No, just a headache. Thanks for the tea.'

Go away, she thought.

He didn't leave. Instead he sat down on a chair and gazed at her, a strange look in his eyes.

'I have a house in town now,' he said after a short silence.

'So I heard.'

Silence again. Amy sipped her tea. Laughter drifted up from downstairs. It seemed to come from far away. She wanted to feel happy again, know joy and fun and laughter, but it seemed out of reach, unattainable, as if it belonged to a different world. She stirred her tea. 'Tanya said you waited a long time before you got the house.'

'Yes. I put in the request as soon as I arrived here.'

'Didn't you like the house in the village?' It was a stupid question. There was nothing to like about that gloomy dilapidated settler's house.

He shrugged. 'I didn't mind it, but it was inconvenient for several reasons.'

He looked so tired. There was something strange about him, but she couldn't put her finger on it.

'Why did it take so long?' she asked.

'That's just the way it goes.' He rubbed his chin and his eyes seemed to look at some non-existent place, somewhere over her shoulder.

'What about Kariuki?' she asked.

'Kariuki? He came to town today to help me move, but he's staying in the village. There'll be another volunteer in the house and he'll probably work for him. I'll find someone else here.'

'Are you all moved in? Did you get it all done today?' She was making conversation—calm, un-emotional words and sentences while everything inside was hurting.

Vic nodded, smiled a little. 'Tanya was there to lend me a hand too. She seems to be of the opinion that a man alone can't cope—arrange furniture, organise a kitchen, that sort of thing. For a supposedly liberated woman she has some pretty antiquated presumptions.'

There was a silence. Again he wasn't looking at her. His eyes seemed dull and lifeless and his shoulders drooped a little. And then suddenly she realised what it was. He wasn't just physically tired; he was mentally exhausted, depressed, and she had never seen him like that. She'd seen him furious, she'd seen him gentle and caring, she'd seen him happy, but not like this, never like this.

'I'm going to have a party,' he said. 'It's about my turn. Maybe we'll roast a goat.'

'Shall I bring something? A salad? A cake?'

'Talk to Tanya.' He smiled, shook his head. 'She's volunteered to organise it all. I take care of the goat and she does everything else. She's a masochist, if you ask me, but she's welcome to the hassle.'

A true volunteer she was, Tanya. In ten or fifteen years she'd be head of some church social, organising bake sales and rummage sales and craft sales and what-ever else needed organising. Oh, damn, Amy thought, I don't want to go to that party, I don't even want to be here. But how was she going to get out of it? Every-body would be there. Maybe she could break her leg, catch chickenpox, something. She finished her tea, put down the cup. Why didn't he leave?

'I have a letter for you,' he said, pulling it out of his breast pocket.

She took it from him, raised her eyebrows as she saw the writing. 'It's from my mother. I just had a letter from her a few days ago.' An awful premonition suddenly washed over her. Something was wrong. She tore at the envelope, ripping it to pieces, pulled out the letter. Her eyes flew across the lines and then she knew.

Her grandfather was dead.

'Oh, no!' she moaned, her eyes filling with tears. The words blurred. She tried to make out the date on the letter.

'What is it?' Vic asked.

She swallowed hard. 'My grandfather ... he died last week.'

'I'm sorry.' His eyes were gentle. 'You knew him well, didn't you?'

She nodded wordlessly. So many happy hours she had spent with him as a child—fishing, hiking, or just talking. He'd been a very special friend to her, colouring her childhood with happy memories.

'Was he very old?'

She stared at him. 'Old? He was eighty-two, but ... but he was always so *alive*, and alert, I never thought of him as *old*.'

Vic smiled. 'Like my grandmother.'

'Yes.'

She remembered his grandmother—a lovely old lady, seventy-nine, but with the spirit and enthusiasm of the young. She was into pottery, astrology, Oriental cooking. Time rolled back and she thought again of that Sunday afternoon when Vic had taken her to meet her. Visions like brightly coloured pictures flashed through her mind—a beautiful drive through sunny countryside to the small town in upstate New York. A charming old house, immaculately clean. Lots of plants, stacks of books. A delicious Sunday dinner. His grandmother, bright, full of fun and laughter, talking about solar energy, deep-sea fishing, the medicinal properties of garlic—anything.

I want to get old like that, she'd thought, not wither away physically and mentally like so many people.

'Thank you for coming with me,' said Vic as he was driving her home that evening. 'I really appreciate it.' His smile warmed her heart, her mind, her body—everything.

'Don't thank me,' she said. 'I had a good time.'

It was dark outside. Red and white lights sparked and shimmered along the turnpike. Amy felt happy, content.

'I visit her once a month or so,' he said. 'But you're the first girl I've ever asked to come with me.'

She looked at him, trying to distinguish his features in the semi-darkness of the car. 'Why? Your grandmother is an interesting person, nice, charming.'

Vic smiled wryly. 'So she is, but most girls I know wouldn't give themselves a chance to find out. Spending half a day with a woman close to eighty seems to most of them a total waste of time.'

Amy shrugged and smiled. 'They don't know what they're missing.'

'Oh, Amy,' he said, grasping her hand. 'You're one in a million.' He slowed down, pulled out at the side of the road, stopped the engine.

'This is the turnpike! You can't stop here!'

'Sure I can—in an emergency.' He pulled her close. 'And this is an emergency. I'll go crazy if I don't kiss you here and now.'

He held her so tightly she could scarcely breathe. Then his lips sought hers in feverish hunger and he kissed her fiercely, passionately, and all she could do was give herself up to it. For a few timeless moments she floated dizzily through heaven.

The feeling was still vivid in her memory. It had been a long time since she'd felt like that. It had been a long time since he'd held her in his arms. But he was here in this room with her—so close and still so far, so unreachable. She glanced at his face, then looked quickly down on her hands in her lap, holding the letter. Why was she always thinking of those past times? Why couldn't she just forget about it? She got up from the bed and walked to the window.

Everything in her life was going wrong, and here she was on the other side of the world and her grandfather was dead, the funeral over.

'I didn't even make it for the funeral,' she said miserably. 'They said I couldn't have made it back in time and anyway, he wouldn't have wanted me to break up my vacation for it.' There were tears in her eyes, rolling slowly down her cheeks. 'He never even wanted a funeral. He once told me he wanted a party instead. He'd had a good life and that was cause for rejoicing, not grieving.' She was crying soundlessly, she couldn't help herself, and she heard Vic get up and stand behind her.

Oh, dear God, don't let him touch me, she prayed.

'It's all right to cry,' he said gently.

She wanted to cry. She wanted to be in his arms and be comforted by him. But comfort was not enough. She wanted his love. But tonight Tanya would be with him and she could not pretend it didn't matter, because it did.

'I'm not crying,' she said thickly. It was silly to deny it, but she couldn't do anything else. His hands were on her shoulders and she couldn't stop herself trembling. Was it because of his touch, or her crying? He hadn't touched her for weeks and she'd lived on dreams and longings and the waiting from Friday to Friday when she'd see him again. She'd nourished her love with memories and hope, but it wasn't enough, it could never be enough.

'Come here,' he said softly, and turned her around and pulled her against him. Something snapped inside

her and she sobbed uncontrollably, giving way to grief
and pain and the crushing fear of losing him. Was she
crying because of her grandfather? Because of Vic?
Both? Her life seemed robbed of all she loved and
treasured, an aching emptiness she couldn't bear.

Her tears spent, she finally quieted down and for a
few moments she stood against him silently. Then she
tried to pull away, but he didn't release her.

'Please, Vic, let me go.' Her voice was still thick
with tears.

'Why?'

'Please.... I didn't mean to break down like that.
I'm sorry.'

'There's nothing to be sorry about.'

Again she tried to pull away and finally he let her go.
She turned her back, not wanting to look at him, not
wanting him to look at her. She blew her nose, dried
her eyes.

'Amy, what's so bad about me comforting you?' His
voice sounded tired.

Because your comfort is not enough!

She shrugged. 'Nothing. But I'm all right now,
really. Besides, they're waiting for you downstairs.'

'I don't care!' he said impatiently. 'What I want to
know is why you act the way you do. Do I repel you or
something? Ever since you came here you've been acting strangely....'

She turned to face him. 'Because I don't want a vacation love affair with you, like you suggested?' Her
voice was cool. She had herself under control again.

'Good God, is that what you're thinking?'

'Shouldn't I? That's what you said once, didn't
you?'

Anger smouldered in his eyes. 'Yes, I did. Because
you made me so damn mad trying to make me believe
you came here on a vacation. I couldn't figure out why.
I still can't.' He jammed his hands into his pockets, regarded her for a silent moment, and sighed.

'Amy, I'm sorry,' he said softly. 'This is not the time to get into an argument.' He touched her cheek lightly. 'Come down with me. You'll get too depressed sitting up here all by yourself.'

His change of mood caught her by surprise. He was so kind and caring, it confused her. It was easier to fight with him, easier to be angry....

'You go ahead, I'll be down in a few minutes.'

'All right.' He left the room, closing the door softly behind him.

Amy took a deep breath, and let it out slowly. I'm going to go down and have another cup of tea, she thought. I'm going to sit there and act like a perfectly happy, normal, well-adjusted person who hasn't a care in the world. One day I'll have my act perfected—I'm getting better at it all the time.

In school at least, somebody loved her. Little Ricky trailed her like a lost puppy. Whenever he had a chance he would crawl in her lap and just sit there, snuggled up close to her. His attachment to her seemed too intense to be normal and it worried her. Something was wrong and it was time to find out what.

'You like hugging and kissing, don't you?' she asked him gently.

He nodded, thumb in his mouth.

'You hug and kiss your mommy and daddy?'

Again he nodded, but said nothing. With his free hand he played with a strand of her hair. 'It's nice,' he said. 'My mommy has hair just like you.'

'Really? Tell me about your mommy.'

'She looks like you. She's nice.'

'Of course she is. I would like to meet her some time.'

He shook his head. 'She's not here now. She's far away.'

An uneasy feeling crept through her. 'Where is she, then?'

He sighed. 'She's in heaven.'

Oh, dear God, Amy thought in honor, tightening her arms around the little body.

'In the new one,' he added.

The new one? Amy thought in bewilderment. She stroked the little blond head, not sure what to say or what to do. Why didn't she know about this? Why hadn't anyone told her? No wonder Ricky had seemed so lost and lonely. No wonder she had never met his mother. Every morning he was delivered to school by his father, a tall, blond American, smiling, handsome. At noon he was collected by his *aya*, a young Kikuyu girl who apparently took care of him.

'Do you talk about it with your daddy?' she asked.

He nodded and took his thumb out of his mouth. 'He says she's coming back.'

Shock silenced her. Then angry indignation welled up inside her. How could he say that? How could he raise the boy's hopes by telling him that?

'Ricky?'

He smiled, lifting his face and kissed her on the cheek. 'I'm going to play now,' he said, and slid off her lap.

The rest of the morning Amy's mind was occupied with Ricky's problem, and she talked about it with Katherine.

'If you want me to, I'll talk to his father,' said Amy. 'Unless you think Linda should do it—she's really his teacher.'

'You do it,' said Katherine. 'Ricky has been confiding in you and it's a touchy situation.'

Amy wrote a note to Ricky's father and gave it to the *aya* when she came to get Ricky at the end of school. She watched them walk down the dusty road, a little blond boy, his hand in that of the African girl, and her heart ached for him.

It was shortly after five when his father came to the door of the apartment, looking tired and worried.

'Your note sounded serious,' he said as he stepped inside on Amy's invitation.

Amy hesitated. 'I think it is. We should talk about it.'

'Let's go to the Outspan and have a drink. I've had a rotten day and I could use one.'

So can I, Amy thought. I'll need all the help I can get with this thing.

He led her to his mini-moke, a crazy little car resembling a box on wheels. She felt as if she were sitting in a bumper car in an amusement park, only she didn't feel very amused.

'Would you mind if I stop at the post office and get my mail?' he asked as he turned the corner.

'No, of course not.'

He parked the car, jumped out and stalked to the boxes, key in hand. She watched him go. He was good-looking, tall, masculine. Then her eyes caught some one else—taller, better looking, more masculine. Vic. Apparently he'd just picked up his mail, too. He came towards her, face expressionless.

'There's nothing for you,' he said.

'I should go in and see if I can get a box myself,' she said. 'I hate to have to bother you with my mail all the time.'

He shrugged indifferently. 'I don't mind.' He looked through his mail without interest, then lifted his head again. 'The party is on Saturday, about three. I don't remember if I told you.'

'I don't think I'll be there.' The words were out before she realised it.

Silence. Cool grey eyes looked at her with a certain kind of speculation. Then he motioned towards Mike who was still standing near the boxes talking to an older man. 'You have better things to do?' There was a hint of contempt in his voice.

She knew what he meant, but refused to acknowledge it. 'I just prefer not to come.'

'It's not very polite to refuse an invitation.' He leaned lazily against the car, looking at her sideways.

'I'm very sorry,' she said coolly. Polite or not, she didn't want to go to that party. Politeness sometimes was a sure road to doom. Politeness had never won a war.

War. Was that what was going on between them? Some kind of emotional warfare? Some strange underground struggle? For what?

'Are you afraid of me?' he drawled.

She caught the glint of mockery in his eyes. *'Afraid? Of you?'*

'That's what I said.'

'You're out of your mind!'

'Am I?'

She saw his face and fury boiled within her. He was laughing. He was *laughing* at her!

Why didn't Mike come back? She wanted to get going. She didn't want to sit there looking at Vic's face any longer. No, she wasn't afraid of him. She was afraid of herself, of her own feelings and reactions.

'Well, if you're not scared, I'll expect to see you on Saturday.' He was still laughing, but didn't wait for her reply. He turned, lifted a hand in greeting to Mike who was coming back, and disappeared around the corner.

So he knew Mike. Everybody seemed to know everybody here. It had its advantages, she supposed.

'Sorry I was so long,' apologised Mike.

'It doesn't matter,' she smiled. 'You know Vic?'

'Sure. Great guy. Works harder than anyone I know.' He started the engine and drove off. 'Don't ask me, though,' he added, 'what a guy like him is doing here as a volunteer.'

I don't have to ask you, she thought. I know.

The Outspan hotel was only a few minutes away and he led her into a room next to the bar, settled her in a chair near the fire and ordered drinks.

'This is a beautiful place,' said Amy. 'I haven't been here before.'

'No? It's a tourist hotel. From here they have tours to Treetops. You've heard of that, haven't you?'

'Oh, yes, it's famous, isn't it? People stay overnight there to watch the animals come to the salt-lick in the night, right?'

He nodded. 'It's all very nice and comfortable. They have dinner there and everything. A lot less tiring than a real safari in the heat and dust.' There was irony in his voice.

The drinks came along with some peanuts and cheese.

'Suppose you tell me what's wrong with Ricky,' Mike said without much preamble.

Amy looked into her glass, searching for the right words. 'I think he misses his mother, mostly.'

'I know,' he said quietly.

'He says I look like her.'

He smiled. 'A little, I suppose. Your colouring— your hair, your eyes. You're taller though.'

'He seems to crave a lot of affection,' Amy said, 'and that's natural, except I don't think it's wise to let him get too attached to me.'

He frowned. 'No, maybe not.' He sighed. 'I'm not really sure how to handle the situation. He's so small and he can't understand it all, and he gets obstinate and angry.'

Amy twirled the ice cubes in her glass. 'What worries me is that he seems to think that his mother is coming back. He says you told him that.'

His eyebrows shot up. 'Yes, I did, of course.'

Amy wasn't prepared for this reply and she stared at him in shock.

'But she isn't.'

'She *isn't?*' His face registered total dismay.

Apprehension flooded through her. Something was wrong, but she wasn't sure what. She took a deep breath and braced herself.

'Where is your wife?' she asked quietly.

'In the States. Going to college, finishing her master's.'

Then she wasn't dead. It had all been some horrible mistake and no wonder she hadn't known about it. She stared at him, speechless.

'What were you thinking?' asked Mike, his blue eyes full of amazement.

She swallowed. 'I ... Ricky told me she was dead.'

'*Dead!* My God, where did he get that idea?'

Amy shrugged helplessly. 'I don't know.'

'What exactly did he tell you?'

She frowned, trying to recall the conversation. 'I told him I would like to meet his mother, and then he said I couldn't because she was far away. And then I asked where she was and he said "in heaven".'

His face changed as if she'd pushed a button. He threw back his head and laughed out loud and all Amy could do was stare at him.

'Oh, good lord, I should have known,' he said. He picked up his glass and finished the last of his drink. 'My wife, Amy, is studying at Yale. Does that mean anything?'

'Yale. Yale, New Haven, Connecticut. *New Haven*. Ricky's words echoed in her mind: *"She's in heaven. The new one."'*

'Oh, no!' she moaned. 'I'm sorry, I'm really sorry.'

Mike smiled and patted her hand. 'Don't worry. It's not your fault. Besides, I'm glad you were wrong. I'm rather fond of my wife.' It sounded like the understatement of the year and Amy gave him an apologetic smile.

'I wonder if I've lost my touch,' she said. 'I'm supposed to see through this sort of thing.'

His eyes gleamed with amusement. 'Have another drink. You look as if you need it.'

'I feel terrible!' she sighed.

'Don't.' He was suddenly serious. 'I'm glad you noticed something was wrong. I'm glad you cared enough to want to talk about it.'

He beckoned a waiter, ordered more drinks. 'Ricky will survive. I know he misses Janice, but it won't be for long,' he commented. 'It was bad timing, my being posted over here, but in some ways it makes it easier for her. With us out of the way she can concentrate better and be finished sooner.' He smiled suddenly. 'Unless of course she wastes a lot of time missing us.'

She wouldn't be surprised. He seemed like a nice man—too nice to be separated from for a long time. But such were the sacrifices of Women's Liberation, she thought ruefully. Yale. Not your average college. Probably his Janice wasn't your average woman, either. A touch of envy prickled her mind. Some women had it all—a lot of brains, a nice man, a cute little kid like Ricky. Oh, well, what do I know? she thought in a flare of optimism. Maybe she's ugly, crosseyed, and mean as a witch.

But somehow she doubted it.

The more Amy thought about it, the more she realised that she'd have to make an appearance at the party— out of pride if not politeness. *'If you're not scared, I'll expect to see you on Saturday,'* he'd said. Well, she'd be there and show him.

I'll show him! It was a thought that kept repeating itself, even while she was eating breakfast the next morning. She became aware, suddenly, that she was shovelling in scrambled eggs with all the energy of someone pitching hay. She put down her fork, picked up her coffee cup and caught Bunny's eyes watching her.

'There's a very unholy look on your face,' commented Bunny. 'Are you planning a murder?'

She's not far off, Amy thought grimly as she watched Bunny pour ketchup on her eggs. 'No,' she answered, 'but what you're doing to your eggs is totally and absolutely disgusting.'

'Don't judge what you don't know,' said Bunny, smiling sweetly. 'However, I do compliment you on your outspokenness. I can see that I have a very beneficial and liberating influence on that tight, neat little character of yours. Give me another month and I'll have you thoroughly rotten, just like myself.'

'Don't count on it.'

'Oh, but I am! You're really making progress. A few weeks ago you would have never said anything derogatory about my eating habits. But things are happening. In that pure little soul of yours, dark things are stirring, I can tell.'

Dark things are stirring all right—bubbling, foaming, fermenting, and one day the cork would pop and everything would come spilling out. She'd felt like that lately, as if indeed inside her some lethal potion was brewing. There were too many bitter feelings, painful thoughts and unanswered questions building up. How much could she handle?

She buttered a piece of toast. Should she ask Bunny what she knew about Vic and Tanya? She could ask her casually, as if she was only curious. She looked at Bunny who seemed very busy eating, but then she looked up, grinned, took a big mouthful of eggs and ketchup, rapture spreading across her face. 'This is really good,' she said, smiling blissfully.

'Bunny, I've been wondering,' Amy began, 'do you know ... I mean, is there....' She panicked and words stuck in her throat.

Bunny stopped eating, her fork in mid-air. 'Is there *what*?'

'Is there anything between Vic and Tanya?' She'd forced out the words, somehow, but she didn't sound casual, not casual at all.

Bunny wasn't fooled, not for a moment. She didn't

answer right away, just looked at her with a thoughtful expression on her face, her eyes empty of the usual laughing sparkle.

'I'm not sure,' she said slowly. 'Tanya talks a lot, but not about that. It sure looks like it sometimes, but I really don't know for sure.' She paused. 'Why don't you ask her?'

'Oh, no!' Amy shrugged. 'I was just wondering.'

'Sure.' Bunny got up and cleared the table, face expressionless. Amy watched her. Bunny had a big mouth, she spoke her mind, but she knew when to say nothing—ask no questions, make no smart remarks.

Ask Tanya, Bunny had said, but it was out of the question. She'd just as soon jump off a cliff. But the idea haunted her. Why was it so impossible? The worst that could happen was Tanya telling her it was none of her business. And knowing Tanya, she'd do it nicely enough.

Sentences formed in her mind. *Tanya, may I ask you a question? Just to make sure I'm not going to throw myself in front of the crocodiles for nothing. . . . Tanya, are you in love with Vic? I'm asking to warn you. Vic will treat you like a car—trade you in for a better model when he gets tired of you. I know from experience.*

Oh damn, she thought. Just *ask* her!

But when Tanya came through the door the day before the party, all thought of what she'd wanted to ask her vanished from her mind. Amy stared in shock at Tanya's hair. The glossy cap had been transformed into a mop of frizzy steel wool.

'Tanya! What have you done to yourself!' she exclaimed.

Wide red mouth smiling, Tanya lowered herself into a chair. 'Don't you like it?'

'I . . . you had such beautiful hair!'

'I was bored and I wanted something else.' She grinned. 'My classes this afternoon were cancelled, so I came to town early and I felt rather reckless, so ... *voilà*!'

Amy sighed. 'It's the style these days, I guess.'

'On most people in this country, it even grows like this naturally,' Tanya said drily.

'That's different.'

'Maybe.' She laughed. 'I can't wait till Monday. My girls will be horrified! Some of them would give an arm and a leg to have straight hair.' She sighed, suddenly. 'I keep telling them they're beautiful as they are, but they keep on trying to straighten their hair and using those bleaching creams on their skin.'

'Well, seeing you may change their minds,' Amy told her.

'Oh, I doubt it very much. They'll just think I'm crazy, that's all.'

In which case Amy could only agree with them, but she didn't say it. Her own hair, long and straight and smooth, might not be the most fashionable, but she couldn't imagine herself with any other hairdo.

'Listen,' said Tanya, 'I need some suggestions for the party tomorrow. Vic has given me a free hand, but I'd better be careful with someone else's money.'

'Is he going to roast a goat?' asked Amy.

'Yes. What else should we have with it?'

'Oh, I guess just lots of salad, some bread and fruit. I don't think anybody is expecting gourmet cooking.'

'No, I suppose not.' Tanya seemed disappointed.

Bunny came home, later than usual, and seeing Tanya's hair exploded into admiration.

Tanya laughed. 'Amy doesn't like it.'

'I didn't say that!'

'You didn't have to.'

'Of course she doesn't like it,' said Bunny. 'She's the more serious type and it wouldn't match her personality.' Grinning, she raked her fingers through her own frizz. 'This magnificent hairdo was specifically created for wild and crazy types like us.'

The banter went on, as it always did when those two got together, and Amy listened to them in a strange sort of detachment. I *am* different, she thought. I couldn't be like that to save my life. *The serious type*, Bunny had called her. No criticism had been implied, she knew, but still she felt strangely inadequate as she listened to the other two. She wasn't sharp or witty like them and she wished she were. It would come in handy sometimes to have something clever to say, but except for a lucky shot now and then, she was incapable of it.

Oh, stop cutting yourself down, she thought suddenly. You're fine the way you are. But it wasn't only that. She hadn't felt exactly capable and in control of her life lately. Ever since she'd come to Africa, as a matter of fact. Her self-confidence was withering away and her peace of mind had fled altogether. I've got to get out of here, she thought despairingly, before I talk myself into a colossal inferiority complex.

Bunny stood up. 'I really have to get out of this filthy uniform. I must have collected a fair share of the world's germs on it today.' She took the stairs two steps at a time.

If I'm going to ask Tanya, I'll have to do it now, Amy thought in sudden panic. It's now or never. She searched for words, and without much thought they were in her mind and everything else was blank and empty.

'Tanya, I want to ask you something.'

'Sure.'

Like neon lights the words stood out in her brain. Blindly she stared at Tanya, not really seeing her, only seeing the words as if they were written on the wall. She swallowed. Her tongue moved and her lips formed the words.

'Tanya, are you in love with Vic?'

CHAPTER EIGHT

The most curious of expressions came into Tanya's eyes, and Amy had no idea at all what went on in her mind. For a few interminable minutes she stared past Amy at the wall behind her. Then her eyes focussed on Amy again and she seemed ready to say something when suddenly she changed her mind and abruptly stood up. She went over to the window and looked out, and all Amy saw was her back and her slightly hunched shoulders.

'Yes,' she said slowly, 'I'm in love with Vic.' Her voice was calm and without much emotion.

Strangely, the answer triggered no reaction in Amy. It wasn't a surprise. Why did I even ask? she thought bleakly. It's been so obvious from the start. All I had to do was look at her face. He sleeps at her house; she stays at his house. He calls her 'something special', she's pretty and smart. How many reasons, how much proof do I need? There was a bitter taste in her mouth and she swallowed, trying to force out some kind of reply.

'I'm sorry, I shouldn't have asked you that,' she said. 'It's none of my business.'

Tanya shrugged, her back still turned. 'Here he comes now,' she said in the same calm and unemotional voice. 'He was in Nairobi today. Maybe you've sold some more pictures.'

Vic strode into the room a few moments later, radiating energy, vitality and an undeniable masculinity. As he saw Tanya's hairdo his lips twisted into a crooked smile and he shook his head.

'Good lord, what you women don't do in the name of beauty!'

Tanya pulled her face into a pout. 'You don't like it?'

'No,' he said bluntly, and grinned. 'But don't worry, you're one of the lucky ones. You're gorgeous no matter how you try to cover it up.'

Tanya frowned. 'Was that a compliment wrapped up in an insult, or an insult wrapped up in a compliment?'

Silvery glints of amusement sparked in his eyes. 'Figure it out and let me know.' Then he turned to Amy, his eyes suddenly cool. 'Have a nice time last night?'

'Last night?' She frowned, then memory returned. 'Oh, you mean....'

He nodded. 'With Mike Saunders.'

He could think what he wanted. If she felt inclined to do so she could have a drink with anybody who would invite her—Prince Charles, Dracula, a Maharajah. It was none of his business.

'Yes, I had a good time.' Irritation sharpened her voice. 'Something wrong with that too?'

His eyes were icy cold now. 'It all depends.'

Amy felt more than saw Tanya looking at them. No doubt she was aware of the less than friendly undertones of their verbal exchange, and Amy didn't like it.

Trying to appear unperturbed, she pasted on a smile. 'Well,' she said airily, 'I'm sure you didn't come here to discuss my social life.'

Before he could answer, Bunny came floating down the stairs, wearing another one of her wild creations.

'Hi there, Vic. Can't stay away from us women, can you? What brings you here?'

'Two reasons. First, I have more money for the artist. Second, we'll have to postpone the party for a week. I have to go to Nakuru tomorrow morning and I won't make it back in time.'

Tanya's face fell. 'But you've already got the goat!'

He shrugged. 'He'll keep. Plenty of grass in the yard.'

Amy stared at him. 'It's *alive*?' she asked, and was

immediately sorry when she saw the mockery in his eyes.

'They usually are before they're slaughtered.'

She said no more. Talk about saying witty things, she thought bitterly. What I do is ask stupid questions.

Bunny and Tanya, however, were in great form today. They dragged Vic into a discussion on politics, and within five minutes they had analysed the world situation, torn it apart and built it up into some Utopia of their own design, all with sharp insight, keen intelligence and a liberal dose of humour.

Apparently Vic had noticed that Amy took no part in their little exercise. 'Why are you so quiet?' he asked.

Amy shrugged. 'It's not my level,' she said in a self-derisory tone. 'I can barely hold my own with four-year-olds, and sometimes not even then.'

He laughed without malice, without mockery, then leaned towards her, eyes warm. 'Don't let it get you down,' he said softly, and the expression in his eyes seemed a throw-back to the past and suddenly, unaccountably, she felt like weeping.

The school was her refuge, her sanctuary. Here she belonged. Here she was useful, needed, loved. Here she could sometimes find a temporary relief from her own pain as she got caught up in the problems of her tiny pupils—the lost shoe, the scraped knee, the mommy in 'heaven'.

'You know what you can do, Ricky? You can write your mommy a letter.'

He was sitting on her lap again, thumb in mouth. He shook his head.

'Why not?'

'I don't know how to make words,' he said sadly.

'Oh, but you don't have to. You can make pictures with paint or crayons or scraps of paper. You can show her what you do, or what you think, by making a picture about it.'

He didn't answer immediately, but seemed to consider it. Then he frowned, looking worried. 'What if she doesn't understand? Maybe she only knows words.'

Amy hugged him. 'No, she'll understand. Mommies know all about that kind of letters too.'

He brightened visibly. 'You know how to send it to her?'

'I'll ask your daddy.'

'Will you put it in an envelope and put a stamp on it and everything?'

'Of course.'

'I want you to come to my birthday party,' he said, changing the subject. 'I'm going to be five!'

'That's wonderful. You're sure getting big.'

He sighed heavily. 'Right now I'm only four,' he said, as if being four was a sorry state of affairs, something to be suffered through with patience.

'When's the party?' she asked.

He raised three fingers. 'Three more nights and then it's my birthday. I want you to come. *Please?*' The plea in the blue eyes was irresistible and Amy smiled.

'You'll have to ask your daddy, okay?'

'Oh, I will!'

Mike Saunders seemed a little uneasy with his son's request. 'I'm sure a kids' birthday party is not what you need after you get out of school,' he said to Amy the next morning.

'I like kids, and I like parties.'

He sighed. 'It seems to mean a lot to Ricky.'

'I'll come, and I'll help if you like. We can play games and make it fun.'

His face lit up. 'Would you really? I'm not very good with kids' parties. Haven't had enough experience, I guess.'

The party was a great success and seeing Ricky's happy face was worth a million. When the cake was eaten, the games were played and the children had left, Amy was persuaded to stay and eat hamburgers, Ricky's favourite food. They barbecued them outside on a little *jiko* and when the dark fell Ricky could barely keep his eyes open.

'Would you mind if I put him to bed before I run you home?' Mike asked.

'Of course not.'

'I want both of you to come and sing songs for me,' Ricky said sleepily.'

Amy agreed before Mike could say anything. She sensed his discomfort and smiled. 'It's all right, really.'

Leaving the sleeping Ricky in the care of the *aya*, they left a short while later.

'I don't know how to thank you,' he said as they reached the apartment.

'You don't have to thank me. It was fun, and Ricky had a good time and that's what counts. It's hard not to have your mother there for your birthday when you're so small.'

'Yes.' He shook his head and grinned. 'I don't know how you do that every day. Those kids drove me crazy this afternoon!'

They were still sitting in the car. Should I ask him in for coffee? Amy wondered. It was still early, but Bunny wasn't in. Better not; he might get the wrong impression.

'Listen,' he said. 'I'm really very grateful. May I offer you dinner at the Outspan one night as a gesture of my appreciation?'

'Oh, no, please! There's no need for that!'

'Why not? I'd like to have dinner with you.'

She hesitated. He wasn't that kind, or was he? She searched his face, wondering, and he smiled.

'I know what you're thinking, but I promise you I have no devious intentions. I love my wife, but I've been living like a virtual recluse lately, and an innocent little dinner with some adult companionship would do me good. It wouldn't worry her, and it doesn't have to worry you.'

Very smooth. Or was it maybe the simple truth? Mike had talked of his wife with love and longing, and he didn't really seem the type who went out hunting as soon as his wife was out of sight. 'I try to stay away from married men,' she said with a half-smile. 'Nothing but trouble.'

'Just dinner,' he said, smiling. 'And no trouble. Boy scout's honour.'

The next day was a disaster. Amy woke up with a headache, burned her wrist on the frying pan and when she arrived at school she learned that Linda Muriuki was sick and wouldn't be in.

The first half hour produced a boy with a bloody nose. Children shrieked, blood was everywhere. She took one good look at the boy and decided he'd live. She sent off the hysterical children and, considering the fact that she didn't feel like handling anything, handled the situation with commendable calmness, or so she thought.

From a distance they watched. Everyone was in a state of uproar except the poor victim himself, a little African boy named Kamau. He sat in the grass pinching his nose and stared up into the sky with a distinct lack of interest or excitement. Apparently the occurrence was nothing new to him.

When all had been dealt with, the children calmed down and in their seats in the classroom, Amy poured herself some coffee from a Thermos, and prayed that the rest of the morning would be less eventful. She looked at the children, saw their big eyes stare at her in grave expectation. Right, she thought, better get on with the day.

'We're going to make a flower garden,' she said, 'on that big piece of paper on the wall.' She explained the mechanics of a collage, handed out scissors, smiles, and pats on the head, acting like an automaton, a wind-up doll.

Good God, she thought, *what's the matter with me?* I'm a nervous wreck. But she knew what it was and it made no sense fooling herself. It was Vic's party tomorrow. It was crazy to be so nervous and she had no explanation for it, only knew that it was there, that some awful sense of foreboding had invaded her and no matter what she did, she couldn't get rid of the feeling.

She sighed and picked up a stack of old magazines, mostly English and American ones—*Woman's Own, Woman's Day, Redbook, McCall's.*

'Cut out nice pictures,' she said, talking automatically. 'All the things that belong in a flower garden. Flowers, and bees, and butterflies, and birds.'

I don't have to go to that party, she thought.

Yes, you do, a little voice answered.

'*Well, if you're not scared, I'll see you on Saturday.*' What made Vic think she was afraid of him? What was there to be afraid of at a party like that? Use your imagination, she said to herself. You'll come up with something.

The children were occupied for the moment, happily destroying the magazines with scissors and fingers, cutting and tearing out pictures of ladies in bras, tuna-fish sandwiches, anti-perspirants, and all manner of things that didn't belong in flower gardens.

She shouldn't have stayed in Kenya. People who made a success of their lives didn't linger at the scene of misfortune; they moved on to better things. Better things? How could anything be better if she didn't have Vic? It could only get worse. For a moment she closed her eyes and in that time a girl hit a boy over the head with a magazine and the screaming and fighting that ensued momentarily took her mind off her worries.

'He wanted to *kiss* me,' the little girl protested with fire in her eyes and contempt in her voice. 'It's *disgusting*!'

Right you are, Amy thought. Who said she was the only one with boy trouble? They learned young these days. Five years old and fighting off the boys already. They watched too much television these days. What would they be doing when they were twelve?

'It's nice that you wanted to kiss her,' she said to the little boy. 'But you should only do it when and if she wants to be kissed.'

No reaction. He looked at her stonily, saying nothing.

'Next time, you ask first, okay?'

He glared at the girl. Obviously his manly pride had been sorely wounded. 'I'll never kiss *her* again,' he said with venom in his voice. 'I'm not in love with *her* any more!'

Well, that was a fast affair. One thing about being five, it seemed, was that you could *decide* not to be in love any more. How handy, Amy thought, and sighed. If only that would work for me.

If only, if only.... There were a dozen ways to finish that sentence. If only Vic hadn't left, if only she hadn't come, if only he still loved her, if only Tanya....

As the morning progressed her spirits sank lower, her sense of doom grew heavier and her patience wore thinner. Her head throbbed.

'You look terrible,' said Katherine. The children were running free in the playground and they sat watching them, drinking coffee. 'Don't tell me you're coming down with something too.'

Amy shook her head. 'I don't think so. I just left my patience at home today and I'm in a rotten mood.'

To say the least, she added silently.

She drank her coffee and watched the children, hearing their laughter, wishing she could laugh too.

'I tried something new today,' she said after a while. 'I thought an exercise in cooperation might be in order and I had them make a group collage—a flower garden. Kept them busy for quite a while. They love cutting out pictures.'

'How did it turn out?'

'Terrible. It looks like a junkyard.'

Katherine smiled and shook her head. 'Poor you!'

'It symbolises my day,' Amy shrugged. And my life, she added silently. A whole junkyard full of shattered hopes, unfulfilled dreams, rejected love and lost happiness.

'You don't have to look so devastated,' said Katherine. 'It's only a collage.'

Amy smiled suddenly. 'Well, there *was* a small sign of hope—a gorgeous yellow rose, growing on a box of spaghetti.'

Katherine laughed and stood up. 'Give me your cup and I'll get us some more coffee. And I'll have a look at that piece of art.'

The keyed-up feeling stayed with her for the rest of the day, and a premonition of disaster, indefinable, yet very real, filled her thoughts and mind and heart.

Getting ready for bed that night she stared at her pale face in the mirror, saw her eyes clouded and lifeless, and rebellion came bubbling up from somewhere. She began to brush her hair, hard, vigorously. 'You're not going to let yourself go to pieces,' she told her reflection out loud. *Nothing, nobody, hakuna mtu* was going to keep her down for very long. And if nothing else, she was learning Swahili and that was a victory of some sort. She grimaced at herself. Be positive, her father used to say. Keep your chin up, her mother used to say. Say your prayers, her grandmother used to say. And if all else fails, a friend used to say, climb on the roof and scream.

Only she wasn't the screaming type. Amy thought again of the children's collage and managed a crooked little smile. There was still that yellow rose on that box of spaghetti.

A small grey house in the middle of a large green lawn. Bright sunshine, the smell of roasting meat, voices, laughter. Amy's senses took it all in as she walked up Vic's driveway, almost tripping on her high-heeled sandals. She should have worn jeans and sneakers, but she'd been glad to have an excuse to put on something else for a change, and she knew she looked good in the soft, skimpy little dress of gold and yellow.

In the shade of a big avocado tree a group of people sat on the grass and Amy walked towards them, seeing and feeling that Vic wasn't there. Was he inside the house?

Gunnar Hornsrud saw her coming and waved her over, motioning her to come and join them. Her eyes flicked over the group. She knew everybody. One time or another most of them had passed through Bunny's apartment. She sat down in the grass and sighed.

'It's hot,' she said unnecessarily, lifting the heavy, warm weight of her hair away from her back and shoulders.

'With all that hair you could keep warm in a blizzard,' somebody said.

'Where's Bunny?' Inger asked.

'She's waiting for Jerry. He doesn't know how to get here.' At least that's what Bunny had told her.

Everybody laughed. 'Bull,' one of the volunteers said. 'I gave him a map two days ago.'

Amy looked around the group of laughing faces. What was it they knew and she didn't? Bunny and Jerry. Jerry and Bunny. And then she saw it and it was suddenly clear. Good heavens, she thought, how could I have been so blind? It had been happening right in front of her eyes and she hadn't noticed it. She'd been oblivious to everything around her except where it concerned herself and Vic.

She jumped to her feet. 'I'm going to have a look at the beast roasting,' she said, and walked over to the makeshift barbecue where two men were tending the meat. They were laughing and talking in Kikuyu as they turned the meat and rearranged the pieces on the grill.

Then she saw Vic as he emerged from the house and her heart lurched with unnamed emotion. Their eyes bridged the distance between them and with an effort she tore her gaze away from his dark face, the probing eyes. She turned and walked across the grass to a small tree full of green and yellow fruit. Lemons, she saw. She fingered the fruit, feeling shaky, and knew he was behind her.

'Brave little girl.' His voice was low, taunting her.

She turned and faced him. 'Oh?'

'You came, so I take it you have no fear.'

She looked him straight in the face. 'Do me a favour,' she said coldly, 'explain to me why I'm supposed to be afraid.'

'I haven't quite figured it out.'

'Maybe because there's nothing to figure out.' Her eyes challenged him.

He shook his head slowly, gazing at her intently as if he tried to look into her very soul. 'No,' he said softly, seriously. 'You're afraid of something. Maybe it isn't me, but it's there. I can see fear in your eyes and on your face. And I've seen it many times.'

Her heartbeat lost its rhythm and she clenched her hands into fists. Damn! she thought.

'You imagine things,' she said coolly. She reached out and picked off a large yellow lemon and tossed it from one hand to the other to hide her nervous trembling fingers. Vic took the fruit from her, gently.

'You're nervous, and you're trembling, and no, I'm not imagining things. You've never been very good at hiding your emotions, have you? Your face is like an open book sometimes.'

A helpless fury raced through her. 'So that's why you understand me so well,' she said caustically, and saw him smile, but there was no malice in his features. What was it that he wanted from her?

'I don't understand you at all,' he said calmly. 'I may read your emotions and reactions, but that doesn't mean I know how to interpret them.'

'Some freshman psychology might have helped,' she said sarcastically. She wanted to hurt, lash out at him, but she knew her efforts were futile. As impossible as it was for her to inflict damage on the tall hard length of him, as impossible it was to hurt his iron ego. It was as indestructible as an Egyptian pyramid, and shooting little arrows at it was pathetic and laughable.

He sighed heavily, as if he were dealing with an obstinate child who exasperated him. 'There's always the easy way to get it all straight, Amy.'

'How?'

'Suppose you tell me?'

'Tell you what?'

She saw his face tighten, his eyes darken. 'Amy,' he said between clenched teeth, 'you know damn well what I mean.'

'I do?' She was pushing her luck, she knew, but she couldn't help it. What did he want from her? Did he really expect her to come out and say she was here for one sole reason only? *Him.* No, sir, not a chance.

The frigid stare he threw at her was cold enough to freeze a truckload of chickens and she felt chilled to the bone. He jammed his hands into his pockets and straightened his back, his tall frame hovering over her ominously. He's angry all right, she thought with a mingling of fear and satisfaction. Mad as hell.

There was a menacing silence, punctuated by Vic's icy glare. 'I don't understand what kind of game you're playing,' he said slowly. 'But I warn you, you'd better stop it or you're going to be sorry.' The words were delivered in a quiet tone loaded with threat, and they didn't fail to have their impact.

Stunned and speechless, Amy stared at him as he turned abruptly and walked off.

She went back to the group of people under the avocado tree, trying hard to look bright and unruffled, but it was an almost physical effort to carry it off. Not much later the food was ready and they all loaded their plates and ate. Bottles of wine were passed around and laughter and jokes filled the air. Everybody was having a wonderful time, but all Amy felt was a fearful sense of isolation. She felt alienated from all that was happy and bright, as if no laughter could ever break through her gloomy sense of misery.

Then Vic joined them, sitting across from her, glancing at her with grey eyes that were calm and clear and without any emotion. His anger had apparently gone, but for some reason his cool indifference hurt her more than any amount of fury.

She stood up and walked away. She wasn't going to sit there and stare at him, or have him stare at her, for that matter. Entering the grey house, she looked for the bathroom. It was a very small house, as Tanya had said. The doors in the narrow hallway were open and she saw a bedroom, Vic's she guessed, and another with a sleeping bag spread out on the bed. Her eyes caught a pair of jeans on the chair, sandals on the floor, a red canvas shoulderbag—Tanya's. Her throat closed and she felt like screaming.

The bathroom was very white and very clean and water rushed from the taps when she opened them, both warm and cold. How about that, she thought wryly, he's back in the lap of luxury.

Outside again she started walking around the yard, feeling restless and lost and nervous, wondering why she felt so apprehensive and jittery, as if she were waiting for something to happen, but having no idea what. Maybe she was discovering the dubious blessing of extra-sensory perception. Maybe a natural disaster was

about to strike—an earthquake, a flood, a volcanic
eruption. But after closer thought she had to dismiss
the possibilities as quite unlikely.

Behind the house the lawn stretched for about fifty
yards and changed into a sloping maize field. Amy
stood at the edge of the lawn looking down on the tall
green maize plants and noticed two young girls cutting
down the stalks with their *pangas*. They wore flowered
dresses with gathered skirts and scarves pulled down
low over their foreheads. As if she felt that she was
being watched, one of the girls straightened and threw
a quick glance in Amy's direction. She said something
to the other girl and then slowly, hesitantly ap-
proached Amy.

'Give me water,' she said in stilted English. It
sounded like an order, but the timid look of the girl
belied that it had been intended as such.

'I'll get it for you,' said Amy, and the girl smiled
shyly, lowering long lashes over dark eyes.

The cornfield simmered with heat. They must be
roasting in there, Amy thought. They'd probably been
working there since morning, maybe hadn't had a
thing to eat or drink. There was plenty of food left,
Amy saw, and she got a big plate and loaded it with
meat, tomatoes and pineapple, filled an empty wine
bottle with water and put it carefully into a cardboard
box and carried it back to the girls.

They sat in the grass, waiting for her, looking hot
and exhausted. She put the box in front of them.

'Are you hungry?' she asked in Swahili, and saw
their eyes widen in surprise at the food.

'*Ndio*,' one of them whispered, and nodded. '*Asante
sana!*'

As Amy turned to leave them she saw Vic coming
towards her, strolling along lazily, hands in his pockets.

'What are you doing?' His eyebrows were raised in
question, his gaze travelled from the box to the girls
to Amy.

Amy swung her hair behind her shoulders, swallowed, and tried to steady the crazy trembling of her knees. This is ridiculous, she thought. Why am I shaking like this? All I have to do is lay eyes on him and I go to pieces. Who is he anyway, that he can do this to me? Mr America? Burt Reynolds? The King of Sweden? One look at the tall, muscular frame in front of her, the wide, hard chest and the strong brown arms, made every cell in her body stand to attention, ready to fight. Instant mobilisation to combat the onslaught on her senses.

Only she wasn't sure what she was supposed to defend herself against—love or fear or anger, or all three. But Vic wasn't doing anything. He just stood there, waiting for an answer to a perfectly innocent question.

'They asked for some water and I took the liberty to give them some of your food as well,' she said, her voice defiant, challenging.

What's the matter with me? she thought. What's got into me? Why do I talk like this?

Vic looked at the food without interest, then back at her. 'I see,' he said indifferently, his tone indicating that he couldn't care less.

Something bubbled inside her, a strange emotion she couldn't identify—a burning itch to prickle his calm, unperturbed exterior.

'I hope I didn't commit another crime,' she said, taunting him. She didn't know what made her say it, why she felt the way she did. The issue was trivial and he'd only asked out of curiosity, and here she was acting as if he were making a federal case out of it. Behind her back she twisted her fingers nervously, seeing the impact of her comment as the calmness on his face vanished. His jaw went rigid, his mouth straightened in a hard line and he took one step in her direction and grasped her shoulders in a painful grip. Petrified, she stared into his eyes. Grey and cold like ice, they held hers in a frozen glare. He was very close to her and she could feel the warmth of his body radiating on to her own, smell the faint scent of his skin, and a tremor ran through her.

His fingers dug into her shoulders and his face was dark and taut with desperate frustration.

'*Stop it, Amy*,' he said in a low and ominously threatening voice. '*Just stop it!*'

For the second time that afternoon he left her standing, walking off with long, even strides. Amy stared at the wide expanse of his retreating back. Well, she'd done it, hadn't she? If she couldn't make him love her, at least she could make him good and mad, but it was a bitter victory and it gave her no joy.

Slowly she walked back to the party, noticing the dusk settling among the trees. Somebody was playing a guitar and a clear voice was singing, and she knew it was Tanya. So she can sing, too, can she? Amy thought as she stood listening. One more point for her. She accepted a glass of wine, drank it, and took anther. Where was Vic? Did she care? He'd probably joined the people inside. The chimney was smoking, so there must be a fire going, and she shivered suddenly, feeling the cool air on her skin now that the sun had gone down. She drank another glass of wine, which warmed her a little, and then she noticed that Tanya had left the group and someone else was singing now, a deep, warm melody of love and longing.

Love. It was everywhere, wasn't it? She could never escape it. She noticed Bunny sitting next to Jerry, very close, legs and arms touching. Amy jumped to her feet, wavering slightly. She could stand it no longer. Walking carefully in the dark, she found her way back to the edge of the maize field and picked up the box with the empty plate and bottle. A dozen ears of corn were on the ground next to the box, and she stacked them on top and carried it all back to the house. She walked through the living room into the hall. At the end of it was the kitchen, door open, light on. One step down the hall and Amy caught sight of the two of them, Vic and Tanya, kissing amid the clutter of dirty dishes.

She whirled around so fast she almost dropped the box. She clutched it to her chest, seeing stars for several frightening moments, then put the box on the living room table and almost ran out of the door, back into the pitch black night. She took in a deep breath of cool air, willed herself to be calm and stepped back into the living room.

She didn't want to feel or think, just drown her senses into oblivion, and the wine was handy and plentiful. Several people had already left and the rest were now sitting in front of the fireplace, telling jokes of dubious virtue. Hunched up in a corner, knees pulled up to her chin, Amy watched and listened, but not with any kind of concentration. After several more glasses of wine she noticed that Vic had joined them, but she didn't see Tanya. Looking at Vic didn't seem to bother her now—he was just a blur, like everything and everybody else, blending in beautifully. She seemed to be alone in a cubicle of glass, a vacuum, a void, seeing and hearing as if everything was very far away. Conversation seemed garbled and made no sense, and she laughed softly to herself, putting her head down on her raised knees. I'm safe here, she thought, safe in my little glass box, and nobody can reach me and now I'll sleep for a little while.

How much time had passed? She wasn't sure, but when she raised her head and looked around the room, only a couple of people were left. Maybe they were staying for the night. Amy got up, feeling dizzy and wobbly, and made for the bathroom where she spent a long time running cold water over her hands and wrists and washing her face.

Her legs seemed barely capable of holding her up and she groaned at herself in disgust and frustration. How much wine had she had? There was no way of knowing, but it had been plenty. I'll need some coffee, or I'll never make it home, she thought. I'll collapse in a heap by the side of the road and some poor old little Kikuyu *mama* will stumble over me in the morning, and I'll get buried under a ton of potatoes or a load of firewood. Her mind conjured up a picture of the imaginary incident and she giggled helplessly at herself in the mirror.

She felt better now and with a deep breath she opened the bathroom door. Head high, walking very straight, she was quite sure, she made her way to the kitchen. Passing the guest room she noticed it was empty; no sleeping bag, no clothes, no shoulder bag. Moved into Vic's room altogether, had she? Made more room for the rest of the guests, no doubt. In the kitchen she picked up the kettle and as she was running water into it, she heard someone behind her.

'So that's where you are,' said Vic.

'That's where I am,' she acknowledged cheerfully, smiling at him beautifully. She plonked the kettle on the stove with a little too much noise and frowned as she reached for the matches. It took three tries before the match struck the box and she was able to light the gas. 'I'm making myself some coffee.' She looked up into his dark, unsmiling face. 'With your permission, of course.'

He said nothing. But then he didn't have to, did he? If there was nothing to say, it was better not to say it. Amy smiled to herself. She felt very smart tonight. Maybe not as smart as Tanya, but *quite* smart.

She steadied herself, leaning against the sink, trying to remember what it was she was attempting to do. Coffee, that was it.

'Where's your coffee?' she asked. 'I don't know this kitchen.'

'Here.' He handed her a jar. 'Instant will have to do. You probably won't taste the difference anyway.'

She stared at the jar. 'What difference?'

'Never mind,' he said between tight lips. Then he

moved into action, finding cups and spoons and, taking
the jar away from her fingers, made the coffee.

His authoritative behaviour bugged her. Taking
charge, was he? What did he think? That she couldn't
make coffee? Mr High-and-Mighty thought he had to
show her?

'I can do it myself!' She tried to sound forceful, but
failed miserably. For some reason she found herself
sounding like one of her five-year-olds.... I can tie my
own shoe! I can pour my own juice! I can do it myself!

It was obvious that Vic was not impressed and the
way he looked at her rather disconcerted her. There
was distaste in his eyes as his gaze slowly travelled
down the length of her body draped against the
counter and his mouth curled in contempt. His eyes
came back to her face and looked at her squarely.

'You're drunk,' he said with disgust.

She let go of the counter, tried to straighten herself
and appear to have some measure of dignity, but failed
miserably. The floor wouldn't hold still under her
feet and the walls seemed rather wobbly, moving back
and forth precariously. She grabbed the edge of the
counter for support, looking back at him with haughty
indifference.

'So? You want to take advantage of it?' Her words
came rolling out on their own power, hung in the silent
air in frightening isolation. Oh, dear God, had she
really said that?

He took one step in her direction and the expression
on his face shocked her into sober fear.

'Damn you!' he whispered fiercely. 'Damn you!'

She tried to back away, but she was trapped against
the counter.

'No! Please don't....'

'Oh, yes, I will!' He hauled her against him without
ceremony, kissed her hard and with a cold passion that
froze her senses, sobering her more than any amount of

coffee could have ever done. She wrenched her face away, but he didn't let her go. He yanked her out of the kitchen, pushed her ahead of him through the hallway into his bedroom, kicking the door shut behind him with a finality that left nothing to the imagination.

'Please,' she whispered, 'please, Vic, don't.' She trembled with helpless fear as she saw the dangerous glinting of his eyes, the stony mask of rage on his face.

He didn't bother to answer. With one swift movement he caught her and with the hard pressure of his hips trapped her against the wall. With his hands free he began to undress her.

And he knew how. Amy struggled silently, helplessly. Her dress slid to the floor and he picked her up, effortlessly, and dumped her on the bed. She was speechless with a nameless terror, knowing she had no defences against the wild and powerful emotions she had unleashed in him. Please, God, no, she prayed. Not like this. *Please!*

His brown hand reached for his shirt, tore it open, sending buttons flying. He flung it on to a chair without looking. His eyes never left her, and filled with an unholy light they seemed to pin her on to the bed.

'Where is everybody?' she whispered.

'They've all left.'

'But Tanya....'

'She isn't here either.' He laughed coldly. 'You miscalculated, didn't you?'

Suddenly, miraculously, fearless fury surfaced in her, and she jerked herself upright. 'Don't you dare!' she cried out. 'Don't you dare, or I'll scream!'

'Go ahead,' he said coldly. 'I doubt if anyone will hear you. You asked for it, you're going to get it.'

CHAPTER NINE

SHE looked around wildly, but there was no way to escape. Vic was like a wild animal ready to jump his prey. Amy covered her eyes with her hands, unable to watch any longer the violent fury that had taken possession of him. She felt the bed sag under his weight, felt him leaning over her, and a tremor of fear shuddered through her. He moved her hands away from her face, looked down on her, and she closed her eyes against the anger on his face.

'Don't tell me you're afraid,' he said coldly, 'because if you are you've only yourself to blame. You deserve everything that's coming to you.'

'*Deserve?*' Fury fired her tongue. 'That says it all, doesn't it? What did you have in mind? Are you planning to torture me? Make me crawl? Force me into submission?'

To her surprise, he laughed softly and with it some of his rage seemed to dissipate and his body relaxed slightly against her.

'No,' he said slowly. 'I'm going to make love to you.'

'*Love!*' she spat, 'you call that *love? Rape* is what the word is!' She tried to twist away from him, but the hard bulk of his body held her down firmly where she was.

'Oh, no. We're going to make love, you and I—warm, wonderful, passionate love.' He touched her hair and her face with warm sensuous fingers, the anger and the fury all gone. 'We should have done that a long time ago, Amy.' There was no coldness in his voice now, no coldness on his face.

Panic surged through. *This* she couldn't fight, she knew. If he took her by force it was one thing—she could have stayed icy cold under it, made it no fun for him at all, but if he seduced her with gentleness her resistance would wither away into nothingness.

'Making love takes two!'

'You're right,' he said calmly, smiling down on her. One hand moved down, touching her breast, and she yanked his arm away.

'You think you can *make* me? You think you're so damn irresistible?'

He nodded, smiling a little. 'Sure I am.'

The smugness! The damn arrogance! But he was right, of course. She couldn't fight him, or her own instincts. For a while she could keep herself under control, but not for long.

He shifted his body slightly. 'I'll show you,' he whispered, lowering his head towards hers. He kissed her slowly, with a soft gentle pressure of his lips. There was no anger left in his touch, only a sweet, warm loving that melted away in her all thought of battle. Feeling him so close to her seemed to soothe her anger and fear, draw out the tender, rapturous feelings of love that lay buried inside her, deep down, but ever-present.

Vic raised his head slightly, looked into her eyes with such love and longing, it took her breath away and rushed her blood warm into every cell of her body. She pulled his head down towards her and he kissed her again, then slowly moved down to her throat, her breast, sending her body floating through a sea of sensuous delight.

'Amy,' he whispered against her breast, 'you feel so soft and warm and lovely.... I want you so much, so much....'

His words quivered through her and she clung to him in unconscious abandon, drained of thought and reason, aware only of a deep wondrous love that searched for completion with every cell of her body. A moan escaped her and he looked up, smiling, caressing her lips with a feathery touch of his forefinger.

'How's this?' he whispered. 'Still think this qualifies as rape?' His voice was lightly teasing. There were warm lights in his eyes and he gently stroked her hair away from her face.

Still, the softly spoken words washed over her like an icy cold shower and the pain of reality seared through her. She froze in his arms, every fibre of her being shrinking away from him in shame and anger and utter desolation. She couldn't speak, but a sob escaped her and she saw him looking at her in stunned surprise.

'My God, Amy, what's the matter with you?'

Unexpectedly she came alive with a riotous rage. 'What's the matter with *me*? What's the matter with *you*? What do you think you're doing?'

'I thought we were making love,' he said softly.

'Love? Love doesn't enter into it, does it? All you wanted was to get back at me, seduce me, show your power. Well, now you know! I'm as ... as weak as the next female. You're good, aren't you? A real master of the art!' She broke down, sobbing miserably, and he looked down on her without touching her, without speaking.

'Now you know!' she repeated. 'I can't help myself, so ... so....' She let out another sob, clenching her hands in a desperate attempt to keep control. 'So you go ahead and ... do what you want to, but leave *love* out of it!'

There was a moment of strangely vibrating silence and his eyes were clouded, unreadable.

'No, thanks,' he said, 'I'll pass.'

'Good! Then let me go.'

His anger was back, she could feel, but not the same as it had been, not the violent fury that had radiated from his whole being. He was hard and tense and totally controlled, his face a rigid mask.

'Get dressed,' he ordered, and got up from the bed

and stalked out of the room. Where was he going? Then she heard the shower. A *cold* one? She hoped so. Good for him; he needed it.

Slowly she got up from the bed and slid back into her dress. Where were her shoes? She felt weak and faintly dizzy and she sank down on the bed trying to remember what she'd done with her sandals. At some time or other she'd pulled them off, but she had no idea where.

Everything seemed very fuzzy in her mind. She wasn't sure how she had got here in this bedroom, what exactly had happened during the party—it was all a blur. She sighed, and then something caught her eye and her heart skipped a beat as she stared at the picture on the wall. It was one of her own—the one she had given him as a birthday present. So he had brought it with him when he came and now it was here hanging on his bedroom wall. It was a strangely confusing thought.

He was back in the room, a towel wrapped around his waist. 'Aren't you finished yet?' His voice was cold and impatient.

She jumped up, smoothing her hair back. 'I can't find my shoes. I....'

'Those flimsy white things? They're next to the fireplace.' Vic reached for some clothes. Apparently he wasn't bothered by an over-supply of modesty and didn't care that she was still there. Not that he had any reason not to be comfortable with his own nudity. He had it all—the perfect male body, all sensuous and virile masculinity. Amy couldn't drag her eyes away from him, stared at him, transfixed. He seemed taller and straighter and stronger, all hard muscle and brown skin and dark hair. A desperate longing overwhelmed her and she wanted to touch him again, have his arms around her, feel him come alive again. But he was cold and alien and distant and no touch of hers would warm him now. Her legs trembled weakly and she sank down on the bed. Swallowing nervously, she watched him dress, one part of her wondering why she was still there, why she hadn't left minutes ago.

Watchful eyes scorned her, seeing, knowing, hurting her.

'It's too late, baby,' he said softly, and she knew that he'd read her face and the humiliation stunned her into helpless silence. She lowered her eyes, feeling hot tears welling up once more, and her hair fell forward, covering her face; she wished she could hide for ever, never see him again.

'Get up and make some more coffee,' he ordered, his tone hard and taut.

Amy got up and walked to the door, her legs moving automatically. She went to the living room, found her shoes and walked out the door into the dark, starlit night. There was no need for coffee; all she wanted was to go home. But she'd barely started on her way when the front door opened and the light flooded over her and Vic grabbed her upper arm and yanked her back inside.

'For God's sake, what do you think you're doing!'

She had no energy to fight him. No energy to argue. She felt dazed, and drained of all emotion.

'Answer me!'

'I was going home,' she said tonelessly.

'You were going to *walk* home? At *one* in the morning? Are you out of your mind?'

She shrugged. She didn't care what he said. He could yell at her all he wanted; it didn't matter any more. 'I don't know why not. I know the way. It's not far.' She stared at her feet, the nail polish on her toenails a faint pink blur.

Why am I crying? she thought, surprised herself by the tears that were brimming over in her eyes. I don't feel anything. I'm dead inside.

Vic's hand cupped her chin, lifted her face towards him. 'Why the hell are you crying? What the hell is it that you want?' He let go of her chin and took her by the upper arms and shook her in a sudden furious frustration. 'Why are you doing this to me?' he demanded savagely. '*Why?* Did you come here to torment me? As some kind of revenge?'

Both physically and mentally she was jolted out of her state of lethargic daze.

'*Revenge?*' she whispered incredulously. 'For *what?*'

'For leaving you.'

It took a minute for her to grasp the meaning of what he had said, but his interpretation baffled her. Bewildered, she shook her head.

'No. I knew from the beginning that you were leaving, that you were going to Africa. There was no ... no commitment.'

'Right. You know why?'

'The obvious, I suppose,' she said bitterly. 'You didn't love me.' She looked into his eyes and the grey was very dark, deep and impenetrable. He let go of her and his arms fell by his sides.

'You're wrong, Amy,' he said slowly. 'I loved you very much. I loved you more than I ever loved anyone.'

His use of the past tense had not escaped her. Agony worse than anything she had ever experienced filled her being. She wanted to cry out, but her throat was thick with a mute despair and her tongue lay dry and paralysed in her mouth. *Please* love me now, she wanted to cry out. *Please love me again.* But the words didn't come.

Fighting back tears, she turned away. 'You never told me you loved me,' she said in a strangled voice.

'I couldn't, Amy.'

She stared at the fireplace, at the dead fire, half-burned logs, warm ashes. 'Why not?' she whispered.

'I was making a big change in my life. I didn't know what was waiting for me here, how I was going to adjust, what I wanted to do with the rest of my life. It wouldn't have been fair to you to drag you into all those uncertainties.' He sighed. 'You know, Amy, "*I love you*" is more than just three little words. I couldn't tell you because I wasn't able to follow up on it.'

He paused and Amy, still staring at the ashes, tried to understand what he was saying. The silence seemed to last a long time and finally she turned to face him, seeing him stare at her with clouded eyes. His hands were jammed deep into his pockets and he looked oddly tired with deep lines next to his mouth. Why was he looking like that? she wondered. What was he thinking? He didn't seem to see her, his eyes were way off looking at nothing in particular. She couldn't think of anything to say to break the silence and after a few interminable minutes he directed his gaze back to her face. He smiled at her without humour. 'But time passes and situations change and here we are, a different time, a different place.'

Her heart contracted. 'Yes,' she said tonelessly, 'I know.'

There was nothing more to say. Vic had loved her once, but he had given her up for a new life and there was no room in it for her now. Maybe in Tanya he had found someone who suited his new life better, or maybe they had just a passing affair like she knew he had had in the past with glossy glamour girls in New York City.

He took her home in the Land Rover and only empty, meaningless phrases passed between them. They said goodnight like strangers and she entered the apartment as quietly as possible. Stepping over faceless, shapeless figures bundled up in sleeping bags on the floor, she moved across the living room and up the stairs.

For hours Amy lay awake, curled up between the sheets, analysing every word Vic had said. *'I loved you more than I ever loved anyone.'* He had meant it, she was sure of that, but maybe love had a different meaning for him. Maybe to him love was something temporary, something that was nice while it lasted, but that could be put aside and forgotten if circumstances required it. Oh, damn, she thought miserably, I feel like a disposable plate, number thirty-seven in a pack of fifty.

A splitting headache and a horrendous thirst eventually drove her out from under the covers and she found some aspirins and drank two glasses of water. When finally morning dawned she silently slipped into the kitched and brewed some coffee. People began to stir and after a while everyone was awake and scrambling for food. Breakfast threatened to be a chaotic affair until Bunny took charge and chased everyone out of the kitchen.

'Sit!' she said, as if she were ordering a pack of dogs. 'Amy and I will fix breakfast, and you guys can clean up afterwards.' Obeying like well-trained terriers, they sat down.

Amy took out cups, put them on a tray and started pouring coffee. 'Hand me the milk, will you?' she asked Bunny.

'Did you have a good time at the party?' Bunny asked with her head in the refrigerator. 'You were walking around like a lost orphan.'

'I had a wonderful time,' Amy lied. 'And I'm surprised you noticed me, or anything else for that matter.'

Bunny straightened, closing the refrigerator door. 'What's that supposed to mean?'

Amy laughed. 'What I noticed about *you* was that

you didn't seem to be very present, so to speak. You were floating around on clouds. I didn't know about you and Jerry until yesterday.'

Bunny began to break eggs in a bowl. She grinned. 'I can't say I've been trying to hide it, but I've noticed your preoccupation with other matters. Actually....'

'So the search has ended?' Amy interrupted. She didn't want to talk about herself.

'Yep. Hope so.'

'Well, he's handsome enough, but what happened to *rich*? He's a *teacher*! How is he going to supply you with all you want out of life—a big house, a swimming pool, travels around the world, etcetera, etcetera?'

'He intends to inherit,' Bunny said gravely. 'His father is in oil.'

'*Oil?*'

Bunny nodded. Her face was solemn, but her eyes were laughing. 'He owns a small gas station in some backwater town in Kentucky.'

Amy was surprised to find there was still laughter left in her. She shook her head. 'I'm afraid that's probably not enough to fulfil all your dreams. What happened to all those standards you set?'

Bunny sighed dramatically. 'I fell in love,' she said with a voice that seemed to indicate that no worse fate could have befallen her. 'You can't have everything. Look what *he's* getting. I'm no bargain, you know. I'm a lousy housekeeper, I'm fifteen pounds overweight, and my dental bills could pay for a trip to the moon.'

'Oh, Bunny, you're crazy!'

'Yeah, that too.'

'Are you alone?' It was Tanya at the door, a few hours later; a Tanya Amy had never seen before—pale, with circles under her eyes and shoulders drooping.

'Everybody is gone,' Amy said, apprehension creeping through her. 'Come on in, sit down.'

Tanya dropped her shoulderbag on a chair, her back turned to Amy. 'I want to talk to you,' she said. Her voice sounded odd and the words lingered on in the room.

'Okay.' Amy didn't know what else to say.

Tanya turned around, facing her. 'I wanted to tell you....' She swallowed. 'Remember you asked me if I was in love with Vic?'

'Yes.'

'May I ask you the same question?'

Amy stared at Tanya, at the blue eyes, dark and troubled, and her hands tightened, her body tensed nervously.

'Are you in love with Vic, Amy?'

She looked away. 'Yes.'

'And you have been for a long time, haven't you?'

'Yes.'

There was a short silence as they looked at each other in hesitant speculation. The secrets were out, the protective barriers down.

'Amy, I wanted to tell you....' Tanya took a deep breath and looked up at the ceiling, her eyes wide in an obvious attempt not to let the tears brim over and run down her cheeks. 'I wanted to tell you that there's nothing between Vic and me.'

Amy stared, swallowed, licked her lips. 'You said you loved him!' Her voice was barely a whisper.

'I do, but he doesn't love me.' Tanya twisted her hands together nervously, and Amy saw slow tears trickling down her face.

'How can you be sure?' she whispered.

Tanya shrugged, a bitter smile touching her lips. 'He *told* me so.' Then again she took a deep breath. 'I never intended to get in your way, Amy. It would have been a rotten thing to do. But I honestly didn't know about you—I mean, I did wonder when you came here, but you didn't stay with him very long and then I thought it was as you said—you were just friends.' She sighed. 'So I went on hoping and dreaming and trying to make him love me too.' She grimaced. 'Making a fool of myself in the process. I *had* to help him move, I *had* to organise that party. I convinced myself he needed me.'

Again a silence filled the room. Amy wanted to say something, *anything*, but she didn't know what. An odd mixture of emotions churned away inside her. It was as if a tornado had hit her wits—all her thoughts and theories and suspicions were shattered to pieces, leaving nothing but chaos in her mind. She looked at Tanya, seeing the pain in her eyes, and a hopeless, helpless sadness emerged from the turmoil inside her.

Tanya gave her a funny, crooked little smile. 'Don't look at me like that, Amy. You don't have to feel sorry for me. I'll live. It's happened to me before, you know. I do this to myself—fall in love with the wrong guys. I'm good at that—falling in love, I mean. What I'm not so good at is falling *out* of it again.' She sighed, still smiling a little. 'You'd think I'd have learned by now—God knows I've had enough practice.'

Amy sank down into a chair. 'Why are you telling me all this, Tanya?'

'I ... I noticed things. Little things going on between you two, and I wondered if it was because of me. And then when you asked me if I was in love with Vic, I knew. The pieces suddenly fitted.' She paused. 'You've nothing to worry about, Amy. He doesn't love me. I wish he did, but he doesn't.'

Amy swallowed nervously. 'He ... stays with you sometimes. I know that.' It took an effort to speak the words.

Tanya smiled bitterly. 'Yes. There's no place to stay overnight for miles around and he often has a lot of work to do in the area. So I offered him my place. I liked his company at first. It's lonely up there and for weeks I don't see a living soul besides the villagers and my students. And then—well, I fell in love with him, even though he never encouraged me.' She grinned through her tears. 'Don't laugh, but all we ever did at night was play cards.'

Amy didn't laugh. She wanted to, but the turmoil in her mind produced a sudden crystal clear image of Vic and Tanya kissing.

'At the party last night. . . .' Amy began, then stopped and swallowed nervously. 'I . . . I saw you in the kitchen.'

'You did?' Tanya bit her lip, looking uncomfortable. 'I'd been drinking, I was desperate . . . I. . . .'

That makes two of us, Amy thought, and suddenly she had the hysterical urge to laugh, but knew that if she started she wouldn't stop. Oh, God, she thought, I'm going crazy, save me from myself.

Tanya straightened her shoulders, looked straight at Amy as if she'd made up her mind she was going to suffer through this with dignity. 'I *threw* myself at him. I'm good at that too, throwing myself at men,' she said, mocking herself now. 'Maybe I should see a shrink and let him figure out what's wrong with me.' She paused, still looking straight at Amy. 'Anyway, Vic untangled himself from my clutches, took me to my room, sat me down and talked to me. *Very* nicely, *very* gently. And that was the end of that.'

Tanya moved away from behind the chair and sat down, letting out a deep sigh. 'And now I'd like a cup of coffee, after which I shall depart.' She smiled bravely.

Amy went to the kitchen, leaned her arms on the counter and let out a deep sigh of her own. '*She's something special,*' Vic had said about Tanya. '*That girl has a heart of gold,*' Bunny had said. Well, it was true, wasn't it?

When Tanya left, Amy impulsively hugged her. 'Thanks for telling me,' she whispered.

Tanya smiled—a small smile, but it was in her face and her eyes and it was real. 'I'm glad I told you. I like you, Amy, and I didn't want to hurt you, really I didn't. And don't worry. I'll survive. Somehow I always do.'

Amy was too exhausted to think straight. It was only three in the afternoon, but after a sleepless night she couldn't stand on her legs any longer. She dragged herself upstairs to her room and collapsed on the bed.

A strange week followed with no sign of Vic, but her thoughts were full of him, day and night, and the things he had said to her kept echoing in her mind. *'I loved you more than I ever loved anyone. But time passes and situations change, and here we are, a different time, a different place.'*

Every excuse she could find would take her to the grocery store, the bank, the post office in the hope to run into him somewhere in town, but she didn't see him, nor did he come to the apartment. She felt as if she had a ten-pound rock in her stomach, her feet were full of lead and she dragged herself through the days with an almost physical effort. *Too late*, her mind kept hammering. *Too late.*

'*Please*,' Bunny begged one morning, 'for *my* sake, do something about yourself! I hate the sight of somebody sinking away in depression. Go jogging, take vitamins—do *something*!' She sighed, gathered up some paperbacks from a pile on the floor and deposited them in Amy's lap. 'Maybe they've got the answer for you. *Read!*'

Amy grimaced as her eyes skimmed the titles. Self-improvement books, all of them. Each pointing their own unique way to health, happiness and peace of mind—meditation, sardines, callisthenics. She moaned involuntarily. No book was going to help her. What she needed was spiritual guidance from a more celestial source, divine inspiration, a vision. Or at least a dog for comfort.

Welcome diversion came when Mike took her out to dinner. She enjoyed his company and was grateful for the chance to talk and think about something else, if only for a few hours.

Every morning Mike spent a few minutes talking to her when he brought Ricky to school, and one day they met in the bakery and he asked her to come for a drink with him. They sat on the terrace of the little restaurant and even before the drinks came Amy knew Mike had something on his mind.

'What's the matter?' she asked.

'Would you believe they're gossiping about us in town? After one lousy dinner?' He was clearly disgusted.

'Well, that didn't take long,' said Amy, resignation in her voice. 'It's a small town and I'm not really surprised, I guess.'

'Does it bother you?'

She sighed in mock despair. 'My life is ruined, my reputation blemished for ever.'

He laughed. 'But not all is lost. You still have your health, and a clear conscience.'

And my virtue, she wanted to add, but didn't.

She stared into her glass. 'Actually,' she said slowly, 'I guess it does bother me a little. It's so *stupid*.' She looked up. 'What about you? What about your wife?'

He shrugged. 'I'm not worried. I've written her about you, how you helped out with Ricky's party, that I took you to dinner. She's not the suspicious type and she knows she has no reason to be. I don't think she'll catch the next plane with a lawyer in tow and demand a divorce.'

'Well, let's ignore it, then. And when your wife comes back I'll invite the two of you for dinner and make sure the world knows about it—put up a sign, take out an ad in the paper. That'll give them something to talk about.'

Mike grinned and shook his head. 'You're really something, you know.'

Yes, sure, she was really something all right, she thought later that night. *Stupid* was the word. No doubt Vic would hear about the so-called romance and all she needed was one more little complication to come between them. Knowing Vic he'd probably come storming in one day and demand an explanation or give her a sermon on the Tenth Commandment.

She didn't have to wait long, but she'd been wrong about one thing: no storm accompanied his entrance. He came wandering in calmly and quietly, looking cool and unperturbed like a lake on a windless day. One look at him and she thought her heart would stop. The rock in her stomach grew five more pounds and her legs began to tremble. I love him, she thought helplessly. Oh, God, I love him so. Her eyes took in every line of his face, his mouth, his calm grey eyes. She hadn't seen him for two weeks and she was hungry for the sight of him.

'How about some dinner?' he asked. 'Or have you eaten already?'

'No. Bunny isn't home, so I was just going to have a sandwich.'

'Okay, I'll take you out. Come on.'

Amy looked down on her jeans and shirt. 'Let me change.'

He took her elbow. 'Not necessary. We're not going to the Outspan.'

No, that was where Mike had taken her and he knew, didn't he? She could hear it in his voice. Don't expect me to take you there, his tone said.

'We're walking,' he said without explanation, and so they did. In one of the side streets they entered a small restaurant where a few men were drinking beer and a young couple were eating dinner. Vic led her to a bare table with a dirty yellow ashtray in the middle. As they sat down Amy heard Vic's chair creak ominously under the weight of his heavy frame and she held her breath.

He's going to go through it and end up on the floor, she thought with curious detachment. But no, to him such an undignified disaster would never happen. Catastrophes of that nature were reserved for people like her. Fortunately her chair made no complaints.

Immediately a waiter came over and took Vic's order.

'You want beer or Coke?' he asked her.

'Coke.'

The waiter retreated and Vic leaned back in his creaky chair, tapping the chipped surface of the table with impatient fingers.

That chair is going to collapse under him any minute now, Amy thought, bracing herself for the crash. Nothing happened.

'How have you been?' he asked.

'Fine,' she replied automatically.

'Made any more pictures?'

'Yes, but I can't sell them.'

'Why not?'

'They're not good. My mind has been on other things.'

'Mike Saunders?'

'No!'

The waiter brought their drinks. Vic picked up his glass and drained it, drinking as if he'd been walking around in Death Valley for the last two days.

'You've been going out with him, haven't you?' he asked quietly, putting down his glass.

Well, there it was, the long-awaited question. And there he was, Virtuous Vic, ready to save her miserable soul from eternal sin.

'Is that why you took me out here? So you could third-degree me about my social life? Why do you bother? What's it to you?'

The corners of his mouth turned down. 'I keep asking myself that. I suppose I keep thinking that one day you, in your infinite impulsiveness, will do something unforgivably stupid and I'll be the only one to help you pick up the pieces.'

For a moment rage paralysed her tongue. 'You ... *Mr Big Shot, Bwana Mkubwa*, what makes you think I even want you around to help me?' Her voice was full of furious contempt.

'I don't know.'

His calm reply took the wind from her sails and she was still searching for some kind of reply when their food arrived, two large plates full of steak, fried potatoes, peas, fried cabbage, cut-up tomato, and all of it topped off with a fried egg and sausage.

Amy gaped inelegantly and Vic laughed at her expression of astonishment. 'Not very sophisticated, but for a poor volunteer it's a good meal for a few shillings.' He ordered another beer and sat back to wait for it. 'You haven't answered my question yet,' he said casually. 'Have you been going out with Mike?'

Amy gritted her teeth. 'Yes. I take it you object?'

He seemed unperturbed by her acid tone and for a moment he searched her face as if he wanted the answer to something, she didn't know what.

'He's married, Amy,' he said quietly.

'I *know* that,' she replied impatiently. Let him think what he wanted; she didn't care any more. She speared a piece of tomato on her fork, but couldn't bring herself to eat it. She examined it instead, counting seeds. She was expecting him to explode any minute now, give her a lecture on morals, but nothing came. Looking up, she saw his eyes and there was no anger, only a kind of weariness she didn't understand. He accepted the beer from the waiter, drank a little, then put the glass down. 'Amy,' he said softly, 'why are you doing this?'

'Doing what? Going out with Mike?' She shrugged. 'Because I want to. I like him and he's ... he's lonely.'

Oh, my, she thought. Why did I say that? He's going to jump on that.

Surprisingly he didn't.

'And you?' he asked gently. 'Are you lonely?'

She stared at her plate and a weariness filled her. 'Yes,' she said quietly. She was tired of covering up her feelings, tired of pretending. Yes, she was lonely, lonelier than she'd ever thought possible. A loneliness that was an aching emptiness inside her and no amount of work seemed to fill it—not her school, not her painting.

Vic reached across the table and took her hand, looking deep into her eyes. 'Why are you doing this to yourself, Amy? It's not going to lead to anything. What happened to the girl I once knew? You wouldn't have touched a married man with a ten-foot pole.'

His touch burned her and Amy pulled back her hand. 'There's nothing between us. We've gone out a couple of times just to talk, about his little boy, mostly, nothing else.' She sounded very calm. She wasn't defending herself, only making a statement.

He said nothing. He was absorbed in thoughts, toying with his food, drinking his beer. He doesn't believe a word of it, Amy thought bleakly. She chewed a piece of meat, had a few peas, but she wasn't hungry and apparently he wasn't either. His mind wasn't on the subject of food, but somewhere way off. She laid down her fork.

'You don't believe me, do you?'

His eyes met hers and he smiled faintly. 'I believe you.'

'What are you thinking, then?'

'You really want to know?'

'Yes.' She almost whispered the words, not knowing why.

'I'm thinking how much you've changed. I wish you were still the girl I used to know at home, the girl I could talk to so well, who understood me.' His eyes held hers in urgent demand. 'What happened, Amy?'

A hopeless, helpless misery engulfed her. *I don't know what happened*, she thought. *I don't understand!* Her throat felt dry and she swallowed.

'I haven't changed, Vic.'

It's you who's changed, she wanted to add, *but I still love you.*

'Yes, you have, Amy. And I don't understand you any more.' He looked almost angry, or was it something else? He picked up his knife and fork and attacked his half-cold steak with a vengeance. Amy tried to eat some more, but couldn't. There was a lump in her throat and her eyes burned. She watched Vic eat. He devoured his food as if he hadn't eaten in days. When he finished he pushed back his plate and drained his beer.

'Why aren't you eating? It's good. There's nothing wrong with this food.'

Frustration welled up inside her. 'I *know* there's nothing wrong with this food! I ... I wish you'd stop saying these things!'

He looked puzzled. '*What* things?'

She sighed. 'Oh, I don't know. Ever since I came here you've been treating me as if you think I don't like anything here, as if I do everything wrong and you blame me for not understanding or knowing everything.'

He looked genuinely surprised. 'Is that what I've been doing?'

'Yes! I know I did some dumb things and made mistakes, but that's only normal, isn't it? You can't expect me to be instantly knowledgeable about a place I've never been to before. It isn't necessary for you to make me feel so ... so stupid, so inadequate all the time!' She took a deep breath. 'And I don't understand why you think I don't like anything—the food, or whatever. I didn't come here expecting all the niceties of American life! Did you think I wanted lobster thermidor, champagne, expensive entertainment? What made you think I cared?' The fork in her hand was trembling and she put it down. 'I ... I came here out of my own free will and of course I didn't know what to expect, but I didn't have to stay, did I? But you, you seem to. . . .'

Again Vic took her hand, covered it with his own, silencing her with his touch. He smiled ruefully. 'It's all right, Amy. I'm sorry.'

She bit her lip, feeling self-conscious and relieved at the same time. 'I'd like some coffee, please.'

The table was cleared, their coffee deposited in front of them. Amy took a sip, but it was too hot and she put the cup down again.

'I'm not the only one who's changed, you know,' she said, staring into the murky depths of her coffee. 'You seemed like a stranger when I arrived here.'

'I knew I would change,' he said quietly. 'No one comes to Africa, lives the way we do and stays the same. I knew it would happen. That's why I wanted to come here.' His eyes darkened and his lips twisted painfully. Again there was that faraway look on his face.

'What's the matter?' she whispered.

'I *had* to go, Amy.'

'I knew that,' she said softly. 'I understood.'

'Did you really?'

'*Yes*. We talked about it. You weren't happy and you had to find out if you couldn't do something more meaningful with your life.'

And I wanted to be part of it, she thought, I wanted to be with you and love you and be loved, but you never said anything. You just left. The pain was still there and it would never go away. She picked up her cup again and slowly drank her coffee.

'Maybe I made a mistake,' he said, and there was so much bitterness in his voice that for a moment she could only stare at him in surprise.

'I don't understand.'

'I loved you, Amy, and when I came here I missed

you terribly. I wanted you with me and I started working out a way so I could ask you. I had plans, Amy, and then everything fell to pieces when you arrived out of the blue.'

It made no sense. No sense at all. She didn't know what to say, but Vic didn't seem to expect any comment and suddenly he pushed back his chair and got to his feet.

'Let's go,' he said in a businesslike voice, as if he dismissed the whole conversation as trivial and serving no purpose.

She sighed and smoothed the hair away from her face. 'I'll pay,' she said on impulse, and reached for her purse.

He frowned. 'I *invited* you to this glamorous place. Why should you?'

'Because I want to. Because I have more money than you have these days.'

He laughed. He actually laughed, and Amy smiled. 'I didn't think I'd ever be able to say that.'

'I bet you didn't,' he said with eyes that had come alive with amusement. 'Okay, rich lady, go ahead and pay. Nobody is going to accuse me of being a male chauvinist pig.'

He stood by while she paid the curious-looking waiter, thumbs hooked behind his belt, and she knew he didn't care, wasn't embarrassed in the least. His ego is as hard as a rock, she thought wryly as they walked out into the street. It was dark and quiet and the shops were closed, but the smell of incense still seemed to linger in the air. Voices drifted through open apartment windows and her ear caught words in Swahili, Kikuyu and Asian languages she could only guess at—Hindi, Urdu, Gujarati. For a few minutes they walked quietly through the cool darkness, then suddenly Vic jammed his hands into his pockets and started walking faster, striding along as if the very devil was at his feet.

'You know, Amy,' he began, picking up a conversation she'd thought had finished, 'I was going to write to you. I was going to write you a long letter to tell you I'd decided not to come back to the States, at least not permanently.' He was looking straight ahead as he was talking and she couldn't see his face. 'I was going to tell you that after I was through with the Peace Corps I was going to find a job overseas—Africa, Asia, Latin America, wherever. And I was going to explain how I felt about what I'm doing. I wanted so much for you to understand me so I could ask you to join me over here. And it wouldn't be an easy life, not for you, not for me, but it would be good and satisfying and meaningful and oh, God, I hoped you'd love me enough to take the risk—to leave your nice, comfortable, secure, safe life and marry me, and then. . . .' He stopped talking. He stopped walking. He turned to look at her, but it was too dark to see much of his face, but she could feel deep, dark, desperate emotions emanating from him and she felt afraid and uncertain by his sudden violent outburst of words.

'And then,' he said slowly, taking her by the shoulders, 'suddenly you were there, right in front of me, and I hadn't had a chance to prepare you. I hadn't had a chance to find us a half-way decent place to live. My first reaction was anger, helpless, hopeless anger because I knew in my gut that everything would go wrong. I thought you'd take one look at the village, one look at that dilapidated house without electricity and spiders all over the walls and you'd run.'

'But I didn't!'

'No! You told me you'd come for a damn *vacation*!'

He turned with so much force that she almost lost her balance when his hands left her shoulders. His words had hit her like a physical blow and she watched

him go in stunned silence. Head down, hands in his
pockets, he was striding along like a man possessed.
She ran after him. In front of the apartment he stopped
and waited for her to catch up with him. There were
so many things she wanted to say, to explain, but she
didn't know where to start, didn't know if he would
ever believe her. Uncertainty choked her and left her
speechless, and for a few moments they stared at each
other wordlessly.

Then she looked away, swallowing hard, and her
eyes caught the light in the living room.

'Bunny is home,' she said tonelessly. She had to say
something. Vic's gaze flicked up to the window, then
down on her. His hands reached out and caught her
face between them.

'Amy, come home with me, please.' There was a
grave, pleading urgency in his voice. 'We've got to talk.
We can't go on like this.'

She felt numb and drained with the effort to think
and her brain was dulled and wouldn't function.
Would any more talking do any good? Could any
amount of explanation bridge the distance between
them?

'Please, Amy.'

As if hypnotised by the tone of his voice, she nodded
and they started walking again, leaving the town and
turning into the dirt road that led past his house. He
was like a shadow next to her, silent, dark, elusive. The
long driveway was pitchblack and full of strange
sounds and shadows, and they were alone in the night
without any other sign of human life around. There
was a dreamlike quality about it all, an illusion of the
senses, as if they had entered a different kind of world
and left reality behind in the bright electric light of
the restaurant. This was a world where words and
explanations were inadequate to reveal the truth. A
truth that could only be perceived by the senses, de-
fined only in terms of pure emotion.

He loves me still.

It was not a thought, not an explanation, not a reason. It was a knowing and a feeling beyond them all. Amy was aware of his dark presence next to her, aware of the love that seemed to quiver in the very air around them. And it was whole and brilliant and beautiful, chasing the dark shadows inside her. She reached out and touched his hand and his fingers closed around hers. The warmth of his touch ran like wine through her blood. Something flowed between them, from him into her and back, and it was more than simple physical contact, it was a meeting of the spirit. She felt alive with a deep warm glowing and there was no reason and no logic and she was nothing more than a weightless creature of emotion.

'I love you so,' she whispered.

'I know,' Vic said quietly. 'I love you too. I always have, I always will.'

They came together in the dark and held each other wordlessly. He felt warm and strong and secure against her and a sense of peace flooded through her and she knew her love was safe.

Something made her look up and between the black tree tops a patch of sky was visible—stars and a half-moon that filtered its silver light among the dark shadows around them.

'Amy,' whispered Vic, his lips stirring her cheek, 'I have something for you.' He moved away from her slightly and reached in his pocket. 'I've carried this with me for a long time.' He held out his hand and on his palm, gleaming in the moonlight, lay a gold wedding band—simple smooth, solid gold. No diamonds or emeralds or rubies. He looked into her eyes with so much love that tears blurred her vision.

'Amy,' he said softly, 'this is a symbol of what I have to offer you: a life and a love that's simple and solid and sincere. No meaningless glitter, no empty sparkle. Only the real thing. I love you, Amy. Will you marry me and share my life? Will you accept this ring?'

She couldn't speak; she nodded with her heart and

Harlequin understands...

the way you feel about love

Harlequin novels are stories of people in love—people like you—and all are beautiful romances, set in exotic faraway places.

Harlequin Romances

The books that let you escape
into the wonderful world of romance!
Trips to exotic places...interesting
plots...meeting memorable people...
the excitement of love....These are
integral parts of Harlequin Romances —
the heartwarming novels read by
women everywhere.

Many early issues are now available.
Choose from this great selection!

Choose from this list of Harlequin Romance editions.*

*Some of these book were originally published under different titles.

Relive a great love story...
with Harlequin Romances
Complete and mail this coupon today!

Harlequin Reader Service

In U.S.A.
MPO Box 707
Niagara Falls, N.Y. 14302

In Canada
649 Ontario St.
Stratford, Ontario, N5A 6W2

Please send me the following Harlequin Romance novels. I am enclosing my check or money order for $1.25 for each novel ordered, plus 59¢ to cover postage and handling.

☐ 422	☐ 509	☐ 636	☐ 729	☐ 810	☐ 902
☐ 434	☐ 517	☐ 673	☐ 737	☐ 815	☐ 903
☐ 459	☐ 535	☐ 683	☐ 746	☐ 838	☐ 909
☐ 481	☐ 559	☐ 684	☐ 748	☐ 872	☐ 920
☐ 492	☐ 583	☐ 713	☐ 798	☐ 878	☐ 927
☐ 508	☐ 634	☐ 714	☐ 799	☐ 888	☐ 941

Number of novels checked @ $1.25 each = $ _____

N.Y. and Ariz. residents add appropriate sales tax. $ _____

Postage and handling $ _____ .59

TOTAL $ _____

I enclose _____

(Please send check or money order. We cannot be responsible for cash sent through the mail.)

Prices subject to change without notice.

NAME _____
(Please Print)

ADDRESS _____

CITY _____

STATE/PROV. _____

ZIP/POSTAL CODE _____

Offer expires November 30, 1981.

103564271